COMMENTS ON THE C

*"Ashton captures the s   es
in three new origina
in characters & settings, makes the mysteries seem like an
extension of the original works. For this reader, Ashton's
stories are like a cool drink of water after a long dry spell."*

*"Hugh Ashton quite simply makes the perfect pastiche. If
you have always wished the original 60 was actually 600,
then his stories are for you. If you want a different Holmes
invading a different era, look elsewhere. But if you want
the originals, buy everything that comes off the
pen of Hugh Ashton."*

*"In writing new stories about the legendary
Sherlock Holmes, Ashton is rubbing shoulders with literary
heavyweights - Neil Gaiman, Kim Newman, Andy Lane
and many others. How does he compare?
Very well, I'm glad to say"*

*"Hugh Ashton continues to grind out masterpieces very
favorably comparable to the original tales by
Sir Arthur Conan Doyle!"*

*"I am not ashamed to admit that I am a Sherlock Holmes
snob. I adore the original Doyle works and it takes a great
deal to impress me. Ashton writes as if channeling
Sir Arthur Conan Doyle himself."*

Also by Hugh Ashton and published by
Inknbeans Press:

The "Deed Box Series" of Sherlock Holmes Adventures

Tales from the Deed Box of John H. Watson MD
The Odessa Business
The Case of the Missing Matchbox
The Case of the Cormorant

More from the Deed Box of John H. Watson MD
The Case of Colonel Warburton's Madness
The Mystery of the Paradol Chamber
The Giant Rat of Sumatra

Secrets from the Deed Box of John H. Watson MD
The Conk-Singleton Forgery Case
The Enfield Rope
The Strange Case of James Phillimore
The Bradfield Push

The Darlington Substitution

(The first three titles are also available bound together in hard covers as a compilation volume: *The Deed Box of John H. Watson MD*)

&

Tales of Old Japanese
Keiko's House
Haircuts
Click
Mrs Sakamoto's Grouse
The Old House

NOTES FROM THE DISPATCH-BOX OF JOHN H. WATSON MD

Notes from The Dispatch-Box of John H. Watson MD: More Untold Adventures of Sherlock Holmes

Hugh Ashton

Published by Inknbeans Press at BarnesandNoble.com, 2013

© 2013 Hugh Ashton and Inknbeans Press

Grateful acknowledgment to Conan Doyle Estate Ltd. for permission to use the Sherlock Holmes characters created by Sir Arthur Conan Doyle.

All rights reserved. Without limiting the rights under copyright reserved above, no part of this publication may be reproduced, stored in or introduced into a retrieval system, or transmitted, in any form, or by any means (electronic, mechanical, photocopying, recording, or otherwise) without the prior written permission of both the copyright owner and the above publisher of this book.

This is a work of fiction. Names, characters, places, brands, media, and incidents are either the product of the author's imagination or are written in respectful tribute to the creator of the principal characters.

www.inknbeans.com

www.221BeanBakerStreet.info

Inknbeans Press, 1251 Sepulveda Blvd., Suite 475, Torrance, CA 90502, USA

Dedication

 HIS BOOK IS DEDICATED to all those who have kept alive in print, on the stage and on film, the memory of the great detective and his faithful companion and biographer.

EDITOR'S NOTES
BY HUGH ASHTON

 HE FIRST DEED BOX sent to me from London containing some of the untold cases of Sherlock Holmes was a source of wonder to me as I explored the various documents within it. When I had come to the end of the cases, though, I confess to having been somewhat disappointed that not all the cases mentioned by Watson in the published works were present. Was it possible, I asked myself, that the box that had been sent to me was not the box that Watson had mentioned in *Thor Bridge*? Perhaps there was more than one box that had been deposited in the vaults of Cox & Co?

As it turned out, my guess was correct. As I was in the final stages of editing *The Darlington Substitution*, I received another message from my friend in the bank in England. Amazingly, another box had been discovered, also with Dr Watson's name painted on the outside. She asked if this should also be sent to me. You may guess at my answer!

EDITOR'S NOTES BY HUGH ASHTON

When the box arrived, I opened it with some excitement, which rapidly turned to an initial sense of disappointment. While the first box had contained neatly sorted papers, for the most part concerned with the cases of Sherlock Holmes, and complete adventures described in a style which required little work before they could be published, the contents of this new box, the physical appearance of which which came far closer to the description of the dispatch-box described by Watson, were different. This box seemed to have been used as a storage place for all Dr. Watson's papers, and not only those relating to Sherlock Holmes. I found myself confronted by laundry lists, old wedding invitations, press cuttings relating to medical colleagues (or so I assumed), and very little which marked John Watson as the intimate friend and biographer of the famous detective Sherlock Holmes.

But my disappointment soon turned to excitement. In the manner of an archaeologist who has dug his way through layers of modern refuse, eventually to discover a Roman mosaic or some similar treasure, I discovered at the bottom of the dispatch-box a cardboard box, stuffed to overflowing with records of Sherlock Holmes and his cases.

To be sure, these papers were in nowhere near the condition that I had discovered the papers in the first of the boxes. Some were rough notes, some were completely contained in notebooks, obviously fair copies which had been intended for publication, but for some reason had never seen the light of day, and there were several packets of loose papers. One of these packets contained many papers written in a hand that I failed to recognise; it being neither that of John Watson, with whose writing

I was now unhappily familiar (" unhappily" on account of its splendid illegibility), nor that of Sherlock Holmes, samples of whose hand I had encountered in the previous box. Of this packet, more below.

Out of these treasures, I have picked three episodes. All of these have connections to the adventures that Watson published.

The first of these is the *Affair of the Vatican Cameos*. This is quite an extraordinary tale, involving as it does low crime and high politics. It also shows to us that Sherlock Holmes was by no means invulnerable. Intelligent and resourceful he may have been for the most part, but this is probably the master detective at his lowest point. Watson, however, does make the excuse for him that he was suffering from a cold, and anyone who has felt their judgement to be similarly impaired by such an infection will sympathise with this.

The next episode that I have picked is puzzling. I have given it the title of the *Reigate Poisoning Case*, although the name that is given here for the major protagonist somewhat contradicts the case associated with that name, as given by Watson in the canon. I have given my thoughts on this confusion in my notes at the beginning of this piece.

The third and final episode that I have chosen to include in this volume is extraordinary. I could hardly believe my eyes when I recognised what I was reading. The name of John Clay is of course familiar to those who have studied the works of John Watson. He is described as " murderer, thief, smasher, and forger" in the Red-Headed League. As I leafed through the pages, I realised that I was reading the story of the " fourth smartest man in London" told in his own words, and his relationship with Sherlock Holmes as his career progressed. I did not have to wonder how this had come into the possession of Dr Watson, as Watson himself has given a complete explanation of these circumstances.

There are still many documents in this box relating to Sherlock Holmes that will repay close examination, and I am sure that in the near future I will be able to release more of John Watson's unpublished works to the world.

For now, please accept the first offerings from the second box of John H. Watson, MD.

Acknowledgements

MANY THANKS TO ALL who have assisted in making this book what it is. No writer is an island—and I am no exception.

First, to my parents, David and Gillian Ashton, who provided me with my love of books and of reading (though my habit of having three books on the go at once, scattered around the house, was probably more of a curse than a blessing). Without this early encouragement, you probably would not be holding this book in your hands today.

For the whole of the last year, Jo, the Boss Bean at Inknbeans Press, has continued to provide her warm words of encouragement and wise advice. I feel very fortunate to have been accepted as a writer by the Beans on the other side of the Pacific Ocean.

Sincere thanks to Mr. Al Basile, whose eagle eyes have spotted errors and infelicities in the early versions of this work, and have thereby helped to improve the book you now hold in your hands.

To my readers and fans around the world (and yes, it seems I do actually have fans, amazing as it still appears to me). Thank you for your encouragement and support.

And as always, to my wife Yoshiko, whose support and assistance make it possible for me to continue in the task of producing these adventures.

NOTES FROM THE DISPATCH-BOX OF JOHN H. WATSON MD

Further Untold Adventures of
Sherlock Holmes

As Discovered By
Hugh Ashton

*To Peter
With best wishes
Hugh T. Ashton
Lichfield 01/21*

The Affair of the Vatican Cameos

EDITOR'S NOTES

The writing I have reproduced here comprised the contents of a small black notebook, written in Watson's hand, and also containing a letter, unique in my experience, the contents and origin of which are explained in the appropriate place. Since there are very few corrections and changes, we may guess that this notebook formed the final manuscript of an adventure that Watson intended for publication. It is not difficult, however, to guess why this adventure never saw the light of day. Almost certainly, Sherlock Holmes would not have been happy to see an account of the humiliation that he suffered as described here. After all, he made his living through his skills as a detective, and for these skills to have been revealed as having been lacking (even though there is some excuse here) would hardly have served as an advertisement for his business.

Even so, this case is of great interest, not only to those who follow the adventures of Sherlock Holmes, but also to those who are interested in the politics of the times in which he lived. This adventure will certainly shed some light on some of the secrets of the British government of the day.

This case is alluded to in The Hound of the Baskervilles. *Holmes says, " I was exceedingly preoccupied by that little affair of the Vatican cameos, and in my anxiety to oblige the Pope I lost touch with several interesting English cases". This is a puzzle to Sherlockians. Was Holmes speaking in some sort of metaphor when he talks about his " anxiety to please the Pope" ? We can see from this account that he was " preoccupied" by the affair— this seems to have been his euphemism for his capture and detention. But was he actually employed by the Pope directly, or does he use His Holiness as a metaphor for the whole Church ? And why would Holmes, who expresses little interest in religion, and so often took cases on their merit, rather than primarily for financial reward, be " anxious" to oblige the Pontiff ?*

The theory to which I am rapidly starting to subscribe is that Holmes was brought up as a Catholic, possibly educated at one of the great Catholic schools of England, such as Ampleforth or Stonyhurst, and to avoid rivalry and comparison with Mycroft, who was almost certainly an alumnus of Trinity College, Cambridge, Sherlock Holmes chose to attend Trinity College, Dublin.

Although such a choice of educational establishment would be far from popular with the Catholic Church, and it is almost certain that Holmes' analytical mind would reject much Church dogma, making him a lapsed Catholic, we may assume that his upbringing left him with some respect for the institution, if not for all its beliefs, which made him utter the words above.

O F ALL THE ADVENTURES I experienced with Sherlock Holmes, few had a more dramatic beginning than the one I relate here.

It was a chill winter's day, and the snow which had fallen all night, and continued to fall still, lay heavy upon London like a shroud. Sherlock Holmes was warming himself crouched in front of the fire, following a fruitless expedition earlier in the morning, during which he had been on the trail of the principal witness in the case of the Tankerville Club scandal.

" The fellow slipped away from me in Bond-street," he complained to me. " It is impossible that he could have known that I was following him, and yet..." He sighed deeply and fell a-coughing. " The wretched cold has seeped into my bones," he declared, and sank down in front of the fire in silence, a posture from which he did not move for a good twenty minutes.

" I had no idea that Trapstall's was now selling throat lozenges," he remarked suddenly. " Have the goodness to pass me one, if you please."

" How did you— ? " I asked.

" Simple. I remarked a copy of *Collier's* as I walked into the room. Since this is not a magazine that is delivered to us by the good Richardson who owns the newsagent's around the corner, I must assume that you walked to Trapstall's, the nearest vendor of the journal to us, to purchase it, a fact that is also demonstrated by the dampness of your overcoat, occasioned by the snow."

" I follow you so far," I said, extending to him the packet of lozenges that I had indeed purchased not two hours earlier at the store. " But these lozenges ? "

" There is really only one way to reach Trapstall's on foot from here, unless you pass by way of the Park, a route that does not recommend itself in this weather. As you know, it is a little hobby of mine to have an exact knowledge of the streets of London, and there is no chemist's or other shop likely to sell these lozenges that lies along that path that you took today. Here in the grate, I see a scrap of the very distinctive wrapper for these patent lozenges, which I know to have been purchased today. Earlier this morning you were complaining of a sore throat and lamenting the fact that there was no medicine here to relieve the symptoms. Ergo, I conclude that you went to Trapstall's, purchased the magazine, and your eye lit upon these lozenges which, if I remember correctly, were not available from there in the past."

" You are absolutely correct," I responded, laughing. " What a far-reaching deduction you have made from such trivial details."

" No detail is trivial," he reproached me, " when it is a question of a crime having been committed. Such so-called 'trivial' details can then easily become matters even of life and of death." He filled his pipe, and was about to light it with a spill, when he flung the flame back into the fireplace. " For once, thanks to this throat of mine, I feel that tobacco would provide little solace."

I glanced at him sharply.

" No, Watson, I am not about to resume my self-poisoning habits. Your concern is duly noted, however." He rose from his cramped position in front of the fire and stretched his long frame. At that moment, the front door-bell rang violently, and shortly after, the door burst open to reveal a man whose height exceeded even that of Sherlock Holmes, but who lacked his wiry musculature. He was dressed well, but given the weather, a little eccentrically, with no overcoat or hat, and I noticed that one of his boots was brown, and the other black. He appeared to be in a state of extreme agitation, which was confirmed when he stopped in the doorway, and gazed wildly about him before his eyes came to rest on Sherlock Holmes.

" You must help me ! " he cried, his eyes fixed on my friend. " My reputation ! My job ! My life ! All ruined ! " So saying, his face turned a ghastly pale colour, and he collapsed in a crumpled heap on our bearskin rug. I bent to succour him, dashing a little water into his face, and forcing a little brandy down his throat when he stirred. At length, he was able to rise unaided and I settled him in an armchair, facing Sherlock Holmes.

" You came from Bloomsbury by cab, of course ? " Holmes asked him.

" Yes, indeed I did so. I felt that it was unwise to incur any delay, such as might be occasioned by public transport."

" You must surely feel the cold outside, after the warmth of the Museum ? "

" I do. My office is well-heated, and today's inclement weather was an unpleasant shock to my system when I stepped outside." He paused, and regarded Holmes quizzically. " I did not inform you of where I work, or from where I came or how, before I... before I lost my wits, did I ? "

Holmes chuckled. " You did not tell me in words, but your dress and other little matters informed me of these things. For example, I see the tip of a season-ticket between Holborn and Parson's Green protruding from your waistcoat pocket. It seems to me to be far more likely that you work close to Holborn and live in Parson's Green than the other way round. As for the cab, you have come here without a hat or a coat, which I would regard as being essential for any type of travel in today's weather, excepting a hansom cab. The fact that your boots do not match tells me several things. Firstly, that you were in a hurry when you put them on." The other nodded. " Secondly, that you wore boots this morning when you went to your place of work, but removed them and wore more comfortable shoes or even slippers there. You do not always do this, but sometimes return home in your lighter shoes, leaving the boots at the office."

" How do you know this ? " asked our visitor.

" One boot is splashed, and the other is relatively clean," Holmes informed him. " Since it snowed this morning, and the snow is still on the ground, indeed, still falling, I assume that you wore a black pair of boots to work, which became wet. However, in your haste to come here, you seized two boots, not caring if they were of the same pair."

" Well, that is all perfectly true," replied our visitor. " And the Museum ? "

" Your appearance, if I may say so, my dear sir, is that of a man who tends to an academic mode of life, rather than a commercial one. Both your physiognomy and your mode of dress mark you out as a man of intellect. Given this, and the fact that a copy of the most recent issue of the *Mémoires* of the *Société des Antiquaires de France* currently protrudes from your pocket, an edition, by the way, which carries a small monograph of mine on the subject of Chaldean systems of mathematics, I drew a bow at a venture, and appear to have hit the mark. However, I confess that I am ignorant of which branch of the museum benefits from your knowledge and expertise."

" You are correct. My name is Avery Pillstone, and I have been in the employ of the British Museum for the past thirty years. For the last five of these, I have held the position of Visiting Curator—a somewhat curious title for one holding a permanent post, but one which is used to describe that member of the Museum's staff who is responsible for the care and safekeeping of those collections and items that are loaned by other institutes. But before we proceed further, there is the delicate question of your fee, should you work on the problem I am about to pose to you."

" My professional charges are on a fixed scale, but there are occasions when I remit them altogether. I do not think you will need to worry yourself unduly about this matter. Judging by your agitation, it would seem that one of the loans of which you have been granted custody is no longer in the possession of the Museum ? "

" That is indeed the case," answered Pillstone. " I refer to the Vatican cameos."

Holmes gave no sign of recognising the objects to which our visitor had referred, and I must have appeared equally blank, for our visitor threw up his hands in the air. " You have never heard of them ? " he exclaimed in bewilderment.

" I live a simple sheltered life, and such works of art are often the furthest things from my mind," smiled Holmes.

" I confess they may be something of an esoteric subject outside the circles in which I move," admitted Pillstone. " I may say that, without boasting, I am reckoned to be one of the first five in the country when it comes to questions regarding smaller artistic artefacts of this type, and I live such a sheltered life, to use your term, Mr. Holmes, that I sometimes fall under the impression that the whole world shares my interest—nay, my passion—in such matters. Why, my dear wife—"

A discreet cough from Holmes interrupted him.

" Many pardons. I tend to become carried away in

my enthusiasms, so I am informed," he said, smiling at his own absurdity. Despite his somewhat comic nature, there was an endearing quality to this unworldly scholar, who reminded me of one of my schoolmasters who had attempted in vain to impart the rudiments of Greek to me, despite his best efforts. " These Vatican cameos," he explained, " are the work of an unknown Italian master of the fifteenth century. They are thirteen in number, and represent Our Lord, together with the twelve Apostles. They were presented by the King of Naples, Alfonso II, to the Pope of that time when the King entered a monastery following his abdication. Since that time, they have remained in the Vatican, and this is the first time that they have ever left Italy. I must confess that I was personally instrumental in persuading the Holy See to allow them to be lent to our Museum, and that after many guarantees and undertakings that the Museum would take responsibility for their safety."

" And now they are missing ? " asked Sherlock Holmes.

" Worse than that," Pillstone told us. " They are missing, and a substitution has been made. And this, on the very day before the cameos were to be placed on public display."

" I see."

" Due to the value of the cameos—the aesthetic and artistic value, that is—we had determined that we place them in a cabinet by themselves in a gallery which would display them to their best advantage, and allowing the public to view them, without the distractions that would be present were they to be shown alongside other works of art."

" And were this loan and the exhibition widely known ? "

" Inside the Museum, yes. It was something of a coup, if I may say so, for us—that is to say, myself—" he added, with a little obvious pride, " —to have made the arrangements for their loan. It is the first time that they have travelled outside the bounds of the Vatican itself, and it required some delicate negotiations for this to happen. However, as you yourself demonstrated to me just now, they are of somewhat specialist interest, and I do not think that the general public has been made aware of the loan. We were planning to place a notice in the entrances to the Museum, informing the public of the exhibition. Naturally, since the cameos have been removed, this course of action has not been followed."

" There has been a substitution made, you say ? "

" You may see for yourself," Pillstone told us, withdrawing a small box from his pocket, and extracting a circular plaque some three inches in diameter from it. He passed the plaque to Holmes, who examined it briefly, and then burst out laughing.

I was puzzled by this, but extended my hand, and Holmes passed the cameo, for such it was, to me. I took one look, and I too was unable to contain my mirth. Carved in a crude but recognisable fashion was a head caricaturing our Prime Minister.

" I apologise for my laughter just now," remarked Holmes. " I am sure that this is not an event calling for merriment on your part, but there is a humorous side to this, provided, of course, that one is not the victim, as is the case with you."

" This was the cameo that replaced the figure of Our Lord in the centre of the display," commented Pillstone.

" The other twelve cameos that replaced those of the Apostles depicted Cabinet ministers and prominent politicians, in much the same style as the one you hold in your hand."

" Were these cameos mounted in any kind of setting ? " asked Holmes.

" They are currently un-mounted, though in the last century they were placed in a gilded gesso frame that was, in the opinion of most experts, hideous. In our display of the cameos at the Museum, we had taken the liberty of placing the Apostles in a sequence to match that of the famous depiction of the Last Supper by Leonardo da Vinci, placing them on a velvet cushion inside the display case."

" Which was locked, naturally ? "

" Of course, with the key being held in my office while I am in the Museum and taken home by me when I return home. There is also a reserve key being held by the janitorial staff. Such reserve keys are themselves held under lock and key, with the Curator and his Deputy alone holding the keys and combination to the safe in which these are held."

" Given the value of the cameos, were any extra precautions made regarding the security of the gallery ? "

" An extra porter would have been placed at the door to the room during visiting hours, but otherwise there were to be no special arrangements in that regard."

" When do you think the substitution was made ? "

" It must have been last night after we closed to visitors. I saw the cameos in the case before I left the Museum yesterday evening, following the closing of the building to the public."

" That time would seem logical. Naturally, the key to the case is still in your possession ? "

" It is. I have a habit of counting the keys on my chain both before and after my journeys to the museum. It is somewhat of a fad of mine, but I am sure you understand my concerns in this matter." Holmes silently nodded his assent. Our visitor continued his narrative. " There is no sign that there has been any attempt to force the lock on either my office door or the desk drawer. I noticed the substitution of the cameos just before we opened the Museum to visitors this morning. I had arrived at the office, had removed my boots, as you observed, Mr. Holmes, and replaced them with the soft slippers that I sometimes wear at work. My feet suffer from the pressure of shoes and boots at times, and it is a comfort to me to be able to wear these slippers, especially on those days when I have no occasion to meet the public. In any event, this inclement weather had caused my boots to become wet, and I had no desire to spend the day in such discomfort.

" Having effected this change, and attended to the correspondence that had come my way, I determined to inspect the items for which I have responsibility. It is my regular habit, as it is of most of us at the Museum, to make such a tour of inspection before the morning influx of visitors. In this particular instance, it being the first day on which the cameos were to be shown, I considered it to be a necessity. As I approached the glass-sided case containing the cameos, I noticed that they did not appear to be precisely in the positions in which I had left them the previous evening. I looked a little more closely, and thereupon realised that the substitution had been made. I returned immediately to my office, retrieved the key to the case, and unlocked it. I removed all the cameos, returned to my office, and instructed my assistant to draft a notice informing the public that the cameos were temporarily not on display. I left the key with him in order that he might put the notice in the case, and close off the gallery pending further investigation."

" Did you inform him of the substitution ? "

" Of course."

" His reaction ? "

" He appeared to be as shocked as I. I had little time to take much note, though, as I was busy changing my boots—in great haste, as you remarked—and I snatched up the central cameo to bring to you."

" Can you give me an idea of the value of these cameos ? "

Pillstone spread his hands in a gesture of helplessness. " That is impossible to say, Mr. Holmes. They are unique, and represent the finest craftsmanship of their age. In terms of purely monetary value, they would be worth many tens of thousands of pounds, given that a buyer could be located. However, as landmarks in the history of art, they are literally without price. Their loss represents a severe blow to the prestige of the Museum—nay, to the prestige of the country which has allowed this to take place." He placed his head in his hands, and appeared to be sobbing.

" Come, man," said Holmes, not unkindly. " From what you tell me, you have little or nothing to reproach yourself for. This theft seems to have been carried out in spite of you, rather than as a result of any action or omission on your part. The first thing we must do is to carry out an inspection of the area. Watson, if you take a hansom with Mr. Pillstone to the Museum, I will be with you shortly."

Y RIDE TO THE MUSEUM with Avery Pillstone was undertaken in near silence, as he sat beside me in the cab, shivering with the cold, and seemingly wrapped in his own thoughts. On our arrival at the Museum, he escorted me through areas usually closed to the public to his office, where a warm radiator seemed to restore his spirits a little.

A younger man, a little under thirty years of age by my estimation, was sitting at a desk to one side of the room, and Pillstone introduced me to him. Pillstone's desk was on the other side, and was slightly larger and more ornate, as befitted his rank. The walls were lined with bookshelves, containing books on art in many languages, and I gazed at them curiously.

" I do not read all these languages fluently," he smiled, " but it is necessary for me to have a smattering of many of them, in order to understand the doings of my colleagues in other countries. Although my field of expertise is the early Renaissance, I have had to make myself a Jack of all trades in order to keep abreast of these developments."

" Would you and the gentleman care for tea ? " asked Pillstone's assistant. " It is about time, and it is no trouble for me to ask for another cup when I collect the teapot from the kitchen."

" An excellent idea, McCoy," Pillstone told him.

" Bring two extra cups, if you please. We are expecting another visitor."

" Certainly, Mr. Pillstone."

Something in the younger man's voice caught my attention, and when he had left the room, I enquired regarding his origins. " Is he from Scotland ? " I asked.

" No, though I, too, was deceived by his voice at first. His family is from Londonderry in Ireland, and they are descended from Scots settlers who arrived there some years ago. When will Mr. Holmes join us, do you think ? "

" I confess that I do not know. He is sometimes a little eccentric in his movements, but almost always arrives at the correct conclusions before anyone else, however late he may be in arriving here."

McCoy re-entered the room, bearing a simple tray, on which stood a teapot and all necessary appurtenances for the production of that most British of beverages. In a few minutes, we were sipping from our cups, when the door opened, and a porter announced the arrival of Sherlock Holmes, who was introduced to McCoy, and declined the latter's offer of tea.

" Thank you," he responded, " but I feel there is little time to waste. Mr. Pillstone, would you have the goodness to show me the case in which the cameos are displayed ? "

" Really ! " exclaimed McCoy in wonder. " Are you really in such a hurry to investigate the matter ? "

" If your Curator was so prompt in securing my services in this matter, the least I can do is to return the compliment by being prompt myself," Holmes replied. " In any event, the longer the scene of a crime is left uninspected, the greater the opportunity for any evidence that may point to the solution of the mystery to disappear. In a case like this, time is of the essence."

" In that event, I will go ahead and ensure that everything is ready for you," said McCoy, starting for the door.

" Very well," said Holmes, but there was something in his voice that was more than mere assent to McCoy's proposal, giving me pause for thought.

" Maybe I will take that tea, after all," he added, as the door closed behind the assistant. He received the cup, and holding it in both hands, moved around the room, pausing at McCoy's desk, and glancing at the papers strewn across its surface. " Most interesting," he remarked, seemingly at random, as he drained his cup and replaced it on the tray. " Come, let us to the cameos."

Pillstone led the way to the gallery in which the cameos had been displayed. The passages through which we passed were not part of the museum that is generally opened to the public, and we met no-one on our journey through these narrow paths, other than two other staff of the Museum, who greeted Pillstone. It was apparent to me that Pillstone had not yet informed these others of the loss.

" Who has access to these passages ? " asked Holmes of Pillstone.

" Typically they are left unsecured. The staff frequently need access to the galleries without disturbing visitors," he responded. " There is little reason for them to be locked, and the exits from them into the galleries are disguised as part of the architecture of the place, so there is little danger of a member of the public accidentally entering."

" And the entrance into the gallery where we are now going ? "

" That is always left unlocked, to the best of my knowledge. Ah, here we are." He grasped a handle, and an almost concealed door swung into the gallery where McCoy was already standing by a large display cabinet by the window. Pillstone ushered myself and Holmes into the gallery, which currently appeared to be roped off, and " out of bounds" to the public. I heard a soft sighing sound as the door of the passage from which we had emerged closed, and I looked behind me. As we had been informed, the door matched the moulding of the general architecture so well that it was difficult to credit the fact that any opening at all existed in the wall.

Holmes had reached the display case, his footsteps echoing through the empty gallery, and was already examining it closely with the aid of the ever-present lens from his pocket, along with a variety of useful tools for assisting him his work. " When was the glass on this cabinet last replaced ? " he asked, straightening up from his inspection.

" Dear me, I have no idea," answered Pillstone. " Before my time, I am sure. In fact, I do not remember the glass on any case in this Museum ever being replaced."

" Excepting that time in the Furniture Gallery when the Austrian gentleman suffered a seizure and fell against the case of Regency exhibits two years ago," McCoy put in.

" Ah, yes, of course. But that would scarcely be germane to this issue, would it, Mr. Holmes ? "

" I hardly imagine so. If you would be good enough to open the case, please, gentlemen ? " he invited.

From his waistcoat pocket, Pillstone produced a

chain, which he examined before selecting a small key. He inserted this key carefully into the lock at the base of the case and pulled, exerting a small effort. The door of the case swung open with a loud creaking sound, and Holmes moved forward, to examine the twelve remaining cameos after first examining the case itself.

" Have you reached any conclusion as to the material of which these replacements are made ? " he asked.

" From a cursory examination, I would say that they are made of glass, and composed of a carved portion glued to the darker surface of the base—a technique we call 'assembled cameo'."

" That would appear to concur with my observations," remarked Holmes, peering through his lens. " And the originals ? "

" Carved from layered onyx, and as such almost irreplaceable. Stone of that quality is hard to come by nowadays."

" Whoever replaced them has a strange sense of humour," replied Holmes. " Come, Watson, and see for yourself."

I stepped to Holmes' side, and examined the twelve caricatures of famous politicians. Most of them were currently members of the Cabinet, but there were a few prominent members of the Opposition among them. All were instantly recognisable, in the style of the newspaper and magazine drawings of the time, and caused me to smile involuntarily as I mentally ascribed names and characters to faces.

" I fear there is little to be learned from these crude pieces, Mr. Holmes," remarked Pillstone.

" Maybe, maybe," remarked Holmes absently, dropping to one knee and examining the floor near the cabinet with his lens. " Aha ! " Withdrawing a pair of tweezers and an envelope from his pocket, he lifted a small object, which I was unable to discern, from the floor, and placed it in the envelope.

" At what hour are these galleries usually cleaned each day ? " he asked.

" After I have departed," replied Pillstone. " McCoy, you usually stay later than I. Do you know ? "

" This gallery is usually cleaned at about half-past six, I believe, sir," McCoy told Holmes.

" Thank you. I believe that is all I wish to see here at present. May we return to your room, Mr. Pillstone ? "

" Certainly. Maybe this time it would amuse you to take the more usual route through the galleries ? "

" That would be most pleasant," Holmes agreed. As he turned to leave, somehow the skirts of his coat managed to catch against the velvet on which the cameos reposed in the cabinet, which had not yet been closed and secured. With a clatter, they fell to the ground, rolling in all directions. Holmes apologised, and bent to pick up the results of his carelessness, but he was forestalled by McCoy, who protested that he would restore order, and would join us directly that was accomplished.

As soon as we had left the gallery, Holmes requested that we return to Pillstone's office by the quickest possible route, declining the invitation to visit various exhibits which the curator felt might be of interest to us. On entering the office, Holmes immediately went to McCoy's desk and dropped to the floor.

" McCoy usually changes his boots for slippers ? " he enquired, pointing to a handsome pair of boots on the floor beside the desk.

" Yes. He took note of my habits and decided to

follow my example. Not every day, but the majority of the time, except on days when we have visitors or must meet the public, of course."

" And yesterday ? "

" I cannot recall."

" Think, man, think ! " Holmes seemed impatient.

" Yes, I do remember now. He was wearing slippers all day."

" And did you leave the Museum before him last night."

" Why, yes, I did. He was working on some correspondence when I left him."

" Thank you. I apologise for my brusqueness just then. I believe I now have some more knowledge regarding the theft."

" And you can return the original cameos ? "

Holmes shook his head. " You may have to wait a little time, I fear, before that happy event transpires," he said. " But have patience. I know I am on the right track."

Naturally, I was fascinated by his words, and wanted to know more about what he had discovered, but knew him well enough to hold my peace. We were joined by McCoy, who reported to Pillstone that all the replacement cameos were now returned to their place, news which was received in silence by the curator.

" We must return now, Watson," Holmes said to me, extending his hand to Pillstone in farewell before repeating the action with McCoy. As he shook hands with the latter, he looked into the other's eyes, and I could not help but observe what appeared to be a look of fear pass across McCoy's face.

S WAS FREQUENTLY THE CASE after Sherlock Holmes had been investigating a crime, he would say nothing to me for the space of at least an hour, during which we returned to Baker-street by cab. Holmes' cough, which was to my mind the result of his exertions earlier that day, continued to worsen, but I held my peace, knowing from experience that he strongly disliked being reminded of any infirmity that might be troubling him.

Twice he took up his pipe, and twice cast it down unlit, seemingly mindful of the discomfort that smoking would cause him, given his current state of health. At length, he spoke to me.

" Now we know the identity of the thief, we must find the cameos."

" You know who took the gems ? "

Holmes shook his head. " Surely it is obvious, even to you, Watson ? Consider the evidence that has come before our eyes. No ? In that case I will explain all later."

I was somewhat nettled by his superior attitude, but held my peace. " But surely the thief will have them at his house ? "

Holmes shook his head. " No, I fear not. If the cameos had simply vanished and not been replaced, I would agree with you. But the replacements have their own significance."

" And what may that be ? "

" Reflect on all those public figures whose images they bear. Of different political parties, maybe, but what binds them all together ? " I was unable to answer the question immediately. " I will tell you," he continued, impatiently. " It is their support, to a greater or less degree, for Home Rule. One point in particular struck me. Are you familiar with the Leonardo painting to which Pillstone referred ? " I shook my head. " The position of Judas Iscariot is that of the fourth from the left. The politician whose caricature occupied that position is Lord D____."

" Who recently announced his support for Home Rule after being staunchly against the idea for so long ! "

" Indeed. A malign sense of humour has cast him as Judas. But my point is that these cameos, I am sure, are the work of an organisation, not of one man. McCoy, having purloined the cameos, immediately disposed of them to a confederate. Of that, I am convinced. We might search him, and every nook and cranny of his dwelling, and we would never discover them. Nor, if we arrested him and questioned him, would we ever learn the truth. It may well be that he is genuinely unaware of the identity of the minds who ultimately lie behind this act, for I cannot believe that he is acting alone in this matter, but has carried out this deed at the behest of a more prominent and powerful individual, possibly heading some sort of organisation that is opposed to Home Rule."

" And what, then," I asked, " is the end to all this ? "

" I fear that is a deep question that I am unable to answer fully at this time. Plainly, a certain amount of embarrassment is to be caused, to our nation as a whole, as well as to the worthy Pillstone. I do not think financial gain is a factor here. As we were told, the cameos are priceless, and the Holy See has no doubt long since renounced the concept of them as having any monetary value. Excepting a secret collector, who acquires works of art in order that he, and he alone, may feast his eyes on them, there would be no sale possible."

" Do such collectors exist outside the realm of legend ? "

" I agree that they are largely creations of the more sensational type of journalist, but I have heard that there are some such, chiefly outside this country."

" So you believe that the aim is to inconvenience the present government and the Vatican ? " I asked.

" To inconvenience them and embarrass them, yes. And, if I may hazard a guess, to drive a wedge between the Holy See and our Government such that Home Rule, which would undoubtedly strengthen the Roman Church in Ireland, would be removed from the Government's agenda for some time to come. This has, I feel, gone beyond the realm of simple theft, and appears to be a matter for the authorities at a level above that of the police force."

" I take it you are referring to brother Mycroft ? " I asked, referring to Sherlock Holmes' older brother, whose influence in the corridors of power was not to be underestimated.

" I have already consulted him briefly while you and Pillstone were travelling to the Museum." Holmes' manner was brusquer than was usual, but I ascribed that to the effects of his cold. He rose from his chair, and started to put on his overcoat and muffler. I rose with the intention of accompanying him. " No, on this occasion, Watson, I do not wish you to be with me. Your presence is typically invaluable, I freely admit, but on this occasion, I prefer to be alone with my thoughts, wherever they may lead me." So saying, he picked up his hat and donned a pair of gloves. " I may be some time, Watson, and will make my own arrangements for dinner. You may choose to dine here or elsewhere."

I was left alone in the rooms at Baker-street as the evening fell, and the lamps along the street were lit. Though Holmes had warned me that he would be late, I strained my ears expectantly for the sound of my friend's foot on the stair. By midnight, he still had not returned, and I took myself to bed, confident that I would meet him at the breakfast table the next morning.

It was not to be. The morning dawned, as damp as the previous day, though the snow had ceased to fall, and there was no sign that Holmes had returned. His hat and coat were missing from their accustomed places on the rack, and when I knocked on his bed-room door and, receiving no answer, opened the door and looked inside, I could see no evidence that he had returned. Though it was not altogether unknown for Holmes to spend all night away from our lodgings when he was engaged on a case, he would generally advise either myself or Mrs. Hudson of his intention to do so.

In addition, the cough from which he was suffering had sounded, to my medically trained ears, to be taking a turn for the worse, and I feared for his health in this inclement weather. When Mrs. Hudson brought the breakfast for two to our rooms, I realised it was superfluous to ask her if Sherlock Holmes had announced his proposed absence to her.

I ate my bacon and eggs in a thoughtful solitary silence, while perusing the morning papers. There appeared to be little of interest there, at least as Sherlock Holmes had taught me to interpret the phrase. There was, I was relieved to see, no report of the theft of the cameos or their replacement, but I assumed, that if Holmes' guess was correct regarding the purpose of the abstraction to be embarrassment of the Roman Church and the British Government, that the thieves would lose little time in announcing the loss.

The hours passed slowly, and time hung heavy on my hands that morning. To say that I was concerned would be an understatement. It was at moments like this that the full depth of my friendship with Sherlock Holmes was apparent, and that the true nature of our companionship revealed itself to me.

By midday, it was hard for me to accept the fact that he was still absent with any kind of equanimity, and I determined to visit the Diogenes Club, despite what Sherlock Holmes had said earlier, in order to enquire of his brother Mycroft what might have become of him. Alas, my trip was in vain. It appeared that Mycroft Holmes had not been seen in the Club that day, and though the porter on duty was sympathetic, and recognised me from my previous visits there, he regretted that he was unable to inform me of Mycroft Holmes' current whereabouts. I left a scribbled note addressed to him, asking for any information that he was willing or able to give me regarding the possible whereabouts of his brother, and left it with the porter.

In the usual run of things, I would have gone to the police and informed them of the fact that my friend was missing, but I did not do so, for two reasons. Firstly, Holmes had informed me that there might be confidential matters involved which were not to be bruited abroad. By informing the police of his disappearance, such information might be picked up by the wrong ears. Secondly, and I will admit that this carried more weight in my mind, I knew full well that Sherlock Holmes would have a deep-rooted objection to any police interference in an affair of this nature. I, as the instigator of such a situation, would undoubtedly be the target of his scorn and contempt, and I had no wish to assume such a role.

I read through the evening newspapers as dusk fell, conscious of the absence of my friend, and my seeming impotence. As the lamps were being lit, the page brought a message, enclosed in an envelope embossed with the name and device of the Diogenes Club. I ripped it open, and read, with some disappointment, the following words, written in a large sprawling hand.

" Dear Doctor Watson,

" I appreciate your concern, which I share, in the matter of the disappearance of my brother. Please believe me and accept my apologies when I tell you that I am unable to give you any further information as to his possible whereabouts. I assure you that I will let you have any information that I possess which I am able to share with you, as soon as such makes itself known to me.

" Cordially yours,

" Mycroft Holmes."*

I need not add that this plunged me into some despair. It was hard for me to sit still in the rooms which reminded me so vividly of Sherlock Holmes' presence, but it was impossible to conceive of leaving to take my meal at a restaurant, or to seek distraction in a music-hall performance or some such.

I had earlier determined not to seek solace in the whisky decanter, but even so, I poured myself a stiff peg before retiring, fancying it would help me sleep. In the event, I passed a troubled night, and arose while it was still dark, having been unable to rest comfortably. The

---

* Editor's note: Amazingly, this very letter was enclosed in the notebook in which the account of this adventure was written, along with the envelope that John Watson describes here.

next day and night, and the next, passed in the same way. There was no news of Holmes, and no word from the police, or from Mycroft, to whom I had sent another message addressed to his club, but from whom I had received no answer.

I took a little comfort from the fact that the police had not contacted me with the news that Holmes' body had been discovered. If an accident had befallen him, I was sure that either Mycroft or I would have been informed. However, it was not likely that his absence was the result of an accident, but I had no idea of where to start a search. It seemed to me in my anxiety that Holmes, whether alive or dead, could be anywhere in all the vastness of London, or indeed, could be in any part of the country. It was not a comforting thought, and I went to bed that evening determined that on the next morning, no matter what the outcome might be, that I would set the police searching for Sherlock Holmes.

Dawn had broken on yet another morning, with the grey slush still covering much of the streets, by the time I had lit the fire, and when I had shaved and made my toilet, I felt ready for my breakfast, having been unable to eat heartily the previous evening, on account of my concern for my friend.

Mrs. Hudson, who from her face appeared to be almost as worried as I regarding Holmes' disappearance, set a tray for one in front of me. I had just poured my coffee, and was about to take the first sip when the door opened, and Sherlock Holmes fairly tottered into the room.

I was amazed at the appearance of my friend. He was pale as death, and dark hollows surrounded his eyes. His forehead was decorated by a large gash, the blood from which was still dripping into his eyes, and there was a purple bruise upon his cheek. He was hatless, and his wet muddy coat was ripped in a number of places. In his hand he carried one half of the walking-stick with which he had left earlier.

" My God, Holmes ! " I cried. " What has happened to you ? "

" Later, Watson, later," he gasped, and coughed, hackingly. " Thank God you are here. I feared you would be absent, searching for me, or engaged in some other similarly foolish endeavour."

I rushed to his side, and assisted him to remove his coat before helping him into a chair by the fire, where he sat, his hands extended to the flames, as his whole body shivered.

" You must change your garments soon," I told him. " And as your friend and as a doctor, I would advise you to retire to bed at the earliest possible opportunity."

" Is that coffee I smell ? " he asked in return, a faint smile hovering about his lips.

" It is, and you shall have it all," I exclaimed, bringing him the cup from which I had been about to drink.

" Ah," he exclaimed, after having drained the cup. " Another dose of the same, and I might begin to feel I was re-entering the land of the living."

" Allow me to dress your wound," I requested. " How did you come by it ? "

" I will tell you of all this later," he told me in a very quiet, hoarse voice. " For now I am very tired, and I wish to rest. But first, if you would, it would be a kindness if you would attend to my wound."

As I bathed and dressed the cut on his forehead, it was apparent that it had been caused by the blow of some blunt instrument, but following Holmes' instructions, I forbore to make further enquiries as to its origin. When I had completed my ministrations, I helped him to his feet and into his bed-room, where I put him to bed. He appeared to fall asleep almost immediately, but I was relieved to note that his breathing seemed easy and regular, though with obvious signs of the cold from which he was suffering. With as much delicacy as I could manage, I withdrew my stethoscope from my medical bag, and placed it against his chest, listening carefully. I was glad to note that there was no detectable congestion of the lungs.

As I emerged from the bed-room, Mrs. Hudson entered. " Did I hear Mr. Holmes come in ? " she asked. " Can I get him some breakfast ? "

I explained his situation to her, suggesting that she prepare a light repast, suitable for an invalid, to be brought in a few hours, and she accepted this suggestion before making her way downstairs.

I propped open the door of Holmes' bedroom, and resumed breaking my fast, with a better appetite now that I knew the whereabouts of my friend, though this was clouded by a natural concern for his well-being. I had picked up the *Morning Post*, and was scanning the agony column, when there was a clatter of boots on the stair.

Without any warning, the door crashed open, and three figures burst into the room. The largest of the men, who stood in front of the other two, was considerably taller than me, and would have presented a formidable figure even had he not been gripping a heavy stick in an aggressive manner. I noticed that a large bruise surrounded one eye, which was almost closed with the swelling, and that the knuckles of his right hand were bleeding. His two companions, though slightly smaller in stature, presented much the same sort of appearance, and likewise bore the marks of battle upon them.

" Where is Holmes ? " asked the leader, for such I took him to be.

" That, sir, is none of your business," I replied, laying down my newspaper, and standing to confront the man. " May I ask what you want with him ? "

" I wish to repay a debt to him, and for him to repay a debt to us," he snarled in surly tones. His two companions laughed unpleasantly at his words, in which I caught an echo of McCoy's manner of speech.

" Then I would suggest that you come back later, alone. It surely does not take three men to repay a debt ? "

" That depends on the manner and the nature of the debt, would you not say ? "

" I fail to take your meaning."

" Then let me make my meaning perfectly clear to you." With these words, he brought his stick down smartly on the table where I had placed the coffee cup and saucer from which Holmes had drunk earlier, smashing the porcelain into a hundred pieces. " Where is Holmes ? " he roared in a voice like thunder, leaning forward and glowering into my face.

I confess that while I am as courageous as the next man, and have been under fire in a savage land facing my country's enemies, this bully and his two accomplices frightened me. " I cannot tell you," I answered him, in as steady a voice as I could manage.

" Cannot tell us, or will not tell us ? " he bellowed.

I was about to answer, when from Holmes' bedroom came the sound of three sharp blasts on a police-whistle.

The three intruders froze in their tracks, and I slipped hastily to the desk and withdrew my Army revolver from the drawer. By the time the three had noticed my movement, the pistol was trained on their leader.

" Drop your sticks," I commanded, as the triple blasts on the whistle sounded again, louder and more confident this time.

" And if we don't ? " sneered one of the accomplices.

" Then I shall shoot you," I told him, as calmly as was possible under the circumstances.

" You would never dare," replied the bruiser, moving forward, stick in hand.

As a doctor, I am sworn to protect the life of others. As a human being, I am obviously anxious to protect my own life. And as a friend of Sherlock Holmes, I was never more determined to protect his well-being than at that moment. I fired my revolver, and the wretch dropped his weapon, clutching at his arm with a sharp cry.

" You _____ ! " he exclaimed, letting loose an obscenity which I will not repeat here.

The other accomplice moved forward, but his leader held him back with a motion of his hand. " Stay back, Jim. This one looks as though he means business."

" Drop your sticks," I commanded once more, and this time was rewarded by the sound of the two remaining sticks falling on the floor. " Now move to the door, with your hands above your heads," I ordered.

As they moved, the whistle sounded once more.

" Confound him ! " complained the leader. " He'll have the law on us if he continues."

" I rather fancy that is his purpose," I remarked.

" Come on, lads, let's run for it ! This cove's too

much of a gentleman," he sneered at me, " to try and shoot us in the back."

Of course, he was correct in his estimate as to my character, and I could only stand mutely as they raced down the stairs and let themselves out into the street, banging the door behind them. Shortly after the echo of the slammed door had died away, Mrs. Hudson emerged from the kitchen and called up to me, enquiring whether Holmes and I required assistance. I was able to assure her that although we had suffered the loss of a coffee cup and saucer, our bodies were as whole as they had been before the invasion.

I hurried into Holmes' bed-room, to find him sitting in bed, seemingly a little refreshed, with the police-whistle still in his hand.

" You played the game superbly, Watson," he said with a faint smile. " If it were not for your courage just then, I am certain that I would be a dead man by now."

" Those men would have killed you ? "

" I have little doubt of it. You heard him say that he owed me a debt ? The black eye and other bruises—I do believe I cracked two of his ribs—and the injuries I inflicted on his friends would provide sufficient justification for my death in their eyes, I fear."

I shuddered. " And the debt they claim from you ? "

Holmes smiled, and for answer reached under his pillow, withdrawing a tobacco tin, and wordlessly handing it to me.

" Handle the contents with extreme care," he told me.

I did as he bade me, revealing a linen handkerchief wrapped around a flat object. I carefully unfolded the cloth, and could not suppress a gasp of astonishment as I withdrew one of the most beautiful objects it has ever been my privilege to handle. It was obviously the head of Our Lord as represented by a true master of artistic creation. The workmanship was exquisite, and the expression on the Face on the cameo was all that we may imagine that of our Saviour to have been—a Face of love and compassion, mixed with an other-worldly strength. I stood in silence, lost in wonder, until I heard a knocking at the door to the rooms.

I passed the cameo back to Holmes, who rewrapped it in the handkerchief and replaced it in the tin. I then moved to the door.

" Who is there ? "

" Sergeant Harris and Constable Wells of the Metropolitan Police. We are responding to the whistle that we heard earlier."

" Enter," I bade the two officers, opening the door to them.

" We believe there was a gunshot fired, sir," the sergeant said to me. " Can you explain this ? "

" Certainly. I fired in self-defence. I was being threatened by three men who had entered uninvited."

" This would be the weapon in question sir ? " indicating the revolver, which still lay on the table. I nodded, and he continued, " And this here ? " as he pointed to the pieces of china scattered on the floor that formed the remains of the coffee cup."

" That is the handiwork of the intruders."

" Did these men give any indication of what they wanted, sir ? Is there any reason for this attack, do you know ? "

" They mentioned something about a debt or debts between them and a friend of mine who is sick in the other room."

" I see, sir. May we have the name of your friend ? "

" My name is Sherlock Holmes," came his voice from behind us. " I remember you, Sergeant, do I not ? I recall you were assisting Inspector Lestrade on a case some time back."

" Well bless me, sir," said the sergeant, obviously delighted at the recognition. " Indeed so, sir. It was an honour to work with you then, and it is an honour to be talking with you now, though I am sorry that it is under such circumstances. Wells," he said, turning to the constable, " take good note of this man. You are looking at the finest detective that England, if not the world, has ever produced. If you ever have the good fortune to work with him, you will learn more from him in five minutes than you will learn from five years in the Force."

" An honour to meet you, sir," replied the constable, who had not spoken until then.

Holmes bowed slightly. " You flatter me, Harris. I am delighted to see you as a sergeant."

" Six months ago, sir, and if I may say so, it was all due to one or two things I picked up from watching you."

" May I ? " asked Holmes, sinking into an armchair. " As Doctor Watson just mentioned, I am somewhat indisposed, and I find it a strain to stand up."

" Of course, sir. Do you feel free to tell us more of the debt that the Doctor here mentioned just now ? "

" I am afraid that is not something that I am able to discuss freely at this time, Sergeant. I am sorry if this appears discourteous, but—"

" No need for an apology, sir. We know that you have

your own business at times, into which it might be unwise for us to enquire too deeply."

" I wish that your superiors would display some of your good sense in that regard," chuckled Holmes. " Watson, it is a cold and raw day. Maybe we should offer our guests some refreshment ? "

" Not while I am on duty, thanking you kindly, sir." He turned to me. " Will you be pressing charges ? If so, I must ask you to come to the station with me and provide a description."

I looked at Holmes and raised an eyebrow, receiving an almost imperceptible shake of the head in return. " No, thank you, Sergeant. I think we will let sleeping dogs lie for now."

" As you wish, sir."

" However," interjected Holmes, " if you could manage to pay more than the average amount of attention to this building on your beat, and pass the word to the others of your colleagues, it would be much appreciated."

The sergeant touched the brim of his helmet. " I'll see what I can manage, sir. Is there anything or anyone in particular we should be looking for ? "

" Any tall well-built men sporting a black eye and speaking with a Scots-Irish accent will repay further study, I believe."

" Very good, sir. I'll pass the word. And a very good morning to both you gentlemen."

" Well ? " I said to Holmes as the sound of police boots disappeared down the stairs. " Should you not be returning to your bed ? "

Holmes yawned. " In just a few minutes. Pray do not fuss over me. I shall live, I have no doubt. First, let me send a telegram to Pillstone."

He scribbled a few words on a piece of paper and rang the bell. Billy the page entered, and Holmes gave him instructions to send the telegram from the post office.

" And now," he announced, " if you would be good enough to wake me up when an answer arrives from Pillstone. I will go to bed again," and suited his action to the words.

I did not have long to wait before the answer arrived. I knocked on Holmes' door, and went in to him. " He will visit us at half-past five, he says. There have been developments of which he will inform us, he says."

" Very good," Holmes answered me, replacing his head on the pillow. " I can see, Watson, that you are consumed with curiosity as to the circumstances that have placed me in this position. Rest assured that I will tell you all at the proper time, which is not, however, now." So saying, he closed his eyes, and I tiptoed out of the room.

At five-thirty, the clocks were striking the half-hour at the precise time that the doorbell rang. Holmes had arisen and made his toilet some time before, and was attired in his usual garments. Nonetheless, the injuries he had sustained to his face were still apparent, and caused Pillstone to start when he noticed them.

" Mr. Holmes ! " he exclaimed. " Are these injuries in any way the result of the enquiries you have been conducting on my behalf ? "

" I am sorry to tell you that they are."

" Please accept my most sincere apologies. When I retained your services, I had no idea that I would be placing you in any kind of danger or risk of violence."

Holmes waved a deprecatory hand. " No matter. Your telegram spoke of a development ? "

" Yes, a most extraordinary thing. McCoy, whom you will remember as my assistant, left work on the evening of the day that you visited the Museum, and has not been seen since then."

" You mean that he has not appeared at work ? "

" Not only that, but he has not even been seen at his lodgings in Camden. He left the Museum, according to the book where we all sign our names, at a quarter past six. When he did not appear at work the next day, I sent a messenger to see if he were ill. The messenger returned bearing the news that not only was he absent from his lodgings, but he had never returned that night. I sent the messenger to Camden again today, and he returned an hour before I left the Museum to come here, and informed me that McCoy had not been seen at all there."

" I am not surprised," remarked Holmes calmly.

" You do not suspect he had something to do with the theft and substitution ? I would be horrified to think that any member of the Museum's staff could be guilty of such an action."

" I am convinced that it was he who was responsible for the actual removal and the substitution of the cameos. However, he was working with a dangerous group of blackguards, but whether his participation was voluntary or forced, I cannot, at this point, say."

" I am shocked beyond words, Mr. Holmes. I treated that young man with every consideration, and would definitely have recommended that he become my successor upon my retirement."

" Well, we all make our errors of judgement, Mr. Pillstone. I hope that the shock I am about to administer to you will prove a more pleasant one, however." So saying, he withdrew the tin containing the linen-wrapped package that I had handled earlier, and offered it to Pillstone. " Open it with great care, Mr. Pillstone," he advised.

The curator demonstrated by his method of handling the object that he was accustomed to such practices, but the joy on his face when he discovered the cameo inside the tin was surely unique. " How can I thank you enough ? This is, of course, the gem of the whole collection, and even if the other twelve were never to be seen again, this alone would almost be sufficient compensation." He paused. " I take it you have not recovered the other twelve Apostles, Mr. Holmes ? "

" Not at present. However, I have every confidence that with your assistance, we will be able to recover them."

" With my assistance ? " cried our visitor, turning pale. " Surely, Mr. Holmes, you are not accusing me of complicity in this appalling act ? "

" By no means," Holmes answered. " All that I meant was that we require your assistance as a member of the Museum staff in baiting the trap that we will set. I have a score or two to settle with these gentlemen, and it would give me the greatest pleasure to see them receive their just deserts in Court."

" Very well," replied Pillstone. " What would you like me to do ? "

" For the next few days, very little. Simply change the notice in your gallery to report that the cameos are being cleaned, or some such, and ensure that your colleagues know that there was some sort of problem in the packing of the cameos when they arrived from Rome which has necessitated this, and which you noticed only the day before they were due to go on display for some time."

" You wish me to give the impression that all the cameos are still in the Museum, but not on display ? "

" Precisely," smiled Holmes. " A certain amount of vagueness as to the exact location of the cameos is advisable, but the impression you must give to others is that they are all under your control, and that they will be exhibited in the near future."

" As it happens, I have already done that. Since I had hoped that your assistance would recover the gems quickly, I did not want to advertise the loss prematurely. I used the reason you have just suggested to explain the delay to their exhibition— that the cameos required a little work to be done before they were ready to be shown to the public."

" Truly excellent. You appear to have anticipated me in all respects. The fact that you can show a selected number of your colleagues the central point of the collection, which I have just given to you, will lend additional strength to your story."

" Indeed it will. I will communicate with you should there be any further developments in the field."

" And I with you. Good day to you, Mr. Pillstone. I do not mean to be discourteous, but," Holmes pointed to his damaged face, " I feel I need a little time for rest."

" Of course. Once again, my thanks to you for your work so far." He gathered up the cameo in its linen wrapping, and left us.

" And I must to bed again," said Holmes. " It is not often that I feel so fatigued, but the last few days have been exceptional in the toll they have taken on my system. Fear not, Watson, you will receive a full account in due course. I have high hopes that the results of this little adventure will be more far-reaching than the worthy Mr. Pillstone can imagine."

THE NEXT MORNING, I WAS AWAKE before Sherlock Holmes and was reading the morning newspapers, when a letter to the editor of the *Morning Post* caught my eye:

" Sir,
" It has come to my attention that the British Museum has recently received a gift of priceless cameos from the Bishop of Rome. I have it on good authority that these gems are intended as part-payment to our government for the country of Ireland, which is to be handed over to the Roman Catholic Church as a dependency to be administered from Rome, following the transfer of further works of art from the Vatican. London is to be excluded from any decisions regarding the country.

" This move will undoubtedly spell the end of the United Kingdom, and I call on all true Britons to resist this treasonous betrayal of our nation."

This was signed with the name of " Sir William Ferguson", a name which was somewhat familiar to me, but which I was unable for the moment to place precisely. I laid the *Morning Post* aside, marking the letter for future reference, and turned to another paper, where to my astonishment, I saw the following:

" THEFT OF VALUABLE VATICAN RELICS

" It was reported last night that thirteen priceless cameos of the 15th century, said to be carved by the master Giovanni Lavatelli, have been stolen from the British Museum, where they were on loan by the courtesy of the Holy See. The authorities at the Museum, led by Mr. Avery Pillstone, the Visiting Curator, who has responsibility for these items, have so far failed to call in the police, fearing that the announcement of the loss of these items will lead to a rift in relations between the British Government and the Vatican."

As I finished reading the piece, Sherlock Holmes walked into the room, fully dressed, appearing to be almost perfectly restored to his former healthy state, other than the bruises and cut on his face that he had sustained.

" See this," I invited, pointing him to the second article.

" Ha ! " he exclaimed, perusing it rapidly, and casting the newspaper to one side. " Has this appeared in any other journal ? "

" Not that I have seen," I said, " but there is this." I passed him the *Morning Post*.

" Sir William at his tricks again," he remarked.

" Who is he ? The name is familiar, but I cannot place him."

" He is a strong Unionist who used to represent an Ulster constituency. He was defeated in the last election, and has been a thorn in the side of the Government since then. This is pure mischief-making, as is the other."

" To what purpose ? "

" They mean to force our hand, it would appear. They know that they have twelve of the thirteen cameos, and this is a challenge to us. Consider. If we fail to produce the cameos as an exhibit on loan from the Holy See, together with the official documentation certifying that they are indeed a loan and not a gift, this adds credence to Sir William's claim that the cameos have been received secretly by the British Government as part of the payment for Ireland by the Catholic Church, or rather by the Vatican, which amounts to almost the same thing. Since he still has twelve of the cameos in this possession, he believes that he is safe in making this accusation."

" I still fail to see the purpose," I objected.

" Sir William entertains the hope that as a result of this story, his followers will rise up against the Irish Catholics, to whose Church, according to him, the island of Ireland has been sold by the British government. Indeed, his object is a civil war."

" But no-one would believe such an outrageous tale ! " I protested. " The whole idea is completely absurd ! "

" There are all too many hotheads in Ireland, as well as on this side of the Irish Sea, who would be all too willing to believe such a story, ridiculous as it might appear to you and me. Those who believe that the Pope is furnished with horns and hooves and a tail and that all Romans are in league with Satan would have little difficulty in swallowing the story."

" And this ? " I asked, pointing to the article in the other newspaper.

" Again, a challenge to us to produce the cameos and prove the writer of the article to be wrong. This particular scandal sheet has a scant respect for accuracy in the articles that it prints, and I am almost certain of the source of this. Even to a more reputable journal, this source might carry some weight, though."

" The source being ? "

Before Holmes could give an answer, Avery Pillstone was announced as a visitor, and the curator entered the room, brandishing a copy of the same newspaper that Holmes and I had just finished perusing.

" Ah, you have seen it too ? " he exclaimed. " This is all the doing of that wretched McCoy ! "

" I had come to the same conclusion myself," replied Holmes. " What leads you to believe this ? "

" This story claims that the cameos are ascribed to Giovanni Lavatelli. There is no-one in the field with any claim to credibility who could possibly believe such an absurdity. I, together with Monsignor Raffaelo of the Vatican, and M. Dulac of the Louvre, am convinced that they can be the work of none other than Pietro d'Angelo. The only person whom I have heard seriously advance the claims of Lavatelli is McCoy."

" Added to which, of course, your name and title are given in the article, and you informed me that none of your colleagues was aware of the disappearance of these articles. The article was obviously the work of someone with extensive knowledge of the workings of the Museum, and there is only one such who fits the bill. How did you come to read this, by the by ? I can hardly imagine that this newspaper is your standard daily fare ? "

Pillstone blushed slightly as he spoke. " It is our cook's choice of literary fare. She was reading this as she was waiting for the kettle to boil, and my name 'leaped out of the page' at her, as she put it. She immediately brought it up to us, in the belief that I would find it of interest."

" There she was not mistaken," said Holmes. " I do not know if you have had time to look at today's *Morning*

Post ? " Pillstone shook his head. " You may find this to be of equal interest."

Pillstone perused the offending letter, his face slowly draining of colour. " Who would believe such a fairy-tale ? " he asked. " This is monstrous ! "

" Watson asked me the same question, and I will give you the same reply that I gave to him. There are all too many, here and in Ireland, who would believe this story to be true, or at least make a pretence of believing it so, as an excuse for carrying out their deeds. Tell me, Mr. Pillstone, did you and McCoy ever discuss religion ? Since you are a Roman Catholic and he is obviously a Protestant, I would imagine that this was a topic of conversation to be avoided."

" How did you know that I am a Catholic ? " exclaimed Pillstone in consternation.

" My dear sir, you cannot expect to have a rosary protruding from your fob pocket and have it ignored." Pillstone glanced down, and hurriedly tucked the article out of sight. " Not that it is any concern or business of mine, you understand, except insofar as it impinges on the problem before us."

" No, it is not a subject that we ever discussed, though I was certainly aware of his beliefs, and I saw no reason to conceal mine. However, I suppose that I should tell you that, despite his undoubted ability in the field in which we were working, there was a definite antipathy between us, which never expressed itself in outright hostility, but which made our relations strained at times."

" I had guessed as much from his attitude towards you when we met. Still, it would appear that our hand has been forced, and we must now play our trump card."

" The genuine cameo, you mean ? "

" Precisely. We must set it in the display case, surrounded by the twelve substitutes."

" But they will deceive no-one."

" We will place them upside down so that the faces are not visible, and you can place a note in the cabinet that the genuine cameos will replace them as soon as cleaning is complete."

" But to what end ? "

" Let us place them so that those who are responsible for the theft will be drawn into the room to examine the cameos more closely, believing the complete set somehow to be now in our possession."

" And then ? " I could not refrain from asking.

" We will have at least one of the gang secured, and we may then discover more through him."

" You seem to be sure this will happen."

" These two newspapers are a challenge thrown down to us. I accept their challenge and welcome it. Let us fight them, but on our own ground and in our own way. But first, I must break my fast, if you will excuse me, Mr. Pillstone. Watson and I will be with you at the Museum within the hour."

Holmes devoured (there is no other word that adequately describes his actions) the excellent meal that Mrs. Hudson brought in to us. " I seem to have eaten almost nothing for the past few days," he said, wiping his lips with his napkin. " Indeed, when I come to consider it, I have indeed eaten virtually nothing for that time. I would be obliged, Watson, if you would be kind enough to step out and replenish my stock of tobacco. I appear to have mislaid my tin, and the supply in the slipper seems to be exhausted. There are one or two matters to which I will attend in your absence."

I left the house and procured the requested article, returning to find Holmes wearing a warm topcoat and carrying his hat, obviously prepared to go outside. He thanked me for the tobacco, but appeared in a hurry to leave.

" Come, let us go to the Museum. I will take my riding-crop with me, I think," referring to the riding-crop he often carried, whose weighted handle was filled with lead and which, in his hands, was a formidable weapon. " In your case, Watson, I feel a revolver would be inappropriate weapon to be used within the confines of the Museum. Would you feel at a disadvantage armed only with an ashplant ? "

" That would depend on the kind of ruffian we are facing."

" You have faced three of them alone before now," Holmes reminded me. " This time we will be two, and I am trusting that we can also rely on the services of at least one of the Museum porters, as well as Pillstone himself, though I confess to doubting his utility in such a circumstance."

We called a cab to the Museum, and were shown to Pillstone's office by one of the porters. " Excellent," exclaimed Holmes, when he saw the thirteen cameos already on the desk. " Let us to the gallery. You have informed your colleagues of the intention to display them ? "

" I did, and though it occasioned some surprise in some quarters, we Curators are pretty independent in the way we are allowed to handle things. I do not think that anyone suspects that there is anything untoward in my deciding to exhibit the cameos at such short notice."

" Let us go, then."

" Through the passages ? "

" If you please, Mr. Pillstone. It may be to our advantage if I am not observed here at present."

Once again, we made our way through the rather cramped, dimly lit passages which formed a secret web honeycombing the Museum (if I may be permitted to mix my metaphors a little) and emerged in the gallery.

" Now," said Holmes, " let us bait the trap." Skilfully, he and Pillstone arranged the genuine cameo and flanked it with the twelve replacements, being careful to place the latter with the caricature portraits facing downwards. Pillstone added a card which explained that these were substitutes, which would be replaced by the genuine article once the cleaning work had been completed. The genuine cameo was clearly visible, and a little separated from the rest. The case was relocked, and Holmes strode to the door of the gallery, cocking his head on one side as he regarded the gems.

" Let us move it so that the cameos are more visible from here," he suggested.

" Very well," replied Pillstone. " Jennings," he called to the uniformed porter standing by the door of the gallery. " Please give us a hand here."

With the four of us, the case was easily rearranged to Holmes' satisfaction. " Thank you, Jennings," he addressed the porter. " Were you in Zanzibar for long ? "

" Ten years, sir," answered the other, and his jaw dropped. " I've never met you before, sir, have I ? Who told you I'd served in Zanzibar ? "

" You did, just now," smiled Holmes.

" I did no such thing ! " the other objected.

" Ah, but my dear Jennings, there are things that you can tell me without words," Holmes informed him.

" Your general carriage marks you out as a military man used to command, and your complexion informs me that you have served abroad, as a member of her Majesty's Army—and have suffered from malaria."

" That's right, sir. The malaria still comes over me at times, and a confounded nuisance it is, to be sure."

" And you were a sergeant, at least. I would guess you held the rank of at least company sergeant-major ? "

The fellow puffed out his chest with a little pride. " Indeed I was that, sir, and I may say without boasting that I was a good one, too. But begging your pardon, sir, how do you know it was Zanzibar where I served ? "

" Your watch-chain, my good Jennings, has attached to it a regimental fob with the name of your regiment and the date of your service inscribed on it. I happen to know that the regiment in question served in the protectorate of Zanzibar when overseas at that date."

" My word, sir, you have sharp eyes and a good knowledge of these things."

" And you also wear a wristband which, if I am not mistaken, is made from elephant hair, and which is commonly believed to bring luck and health. Such are commonly produced and sold in East Africa, are they not, so I would assume that you made at least one trip to the mainland ? "

" Indeed I did, sir. Pardon me, but you're not a part of the Museum staff, are you, sir ? May I ask what you and this gentleman," indicating me, " and Mr. Pillstone are planning ? "

" We are hoping to catch a gang of desperate ruffians who are out to destroy the peace of this nation, Jennings," replied Holmes. I could see that he now had the man's complete confidence, and Jennings would be prepared to follow him into the jaws of hell itself. It was a quality I had remarked in Holmes on previous occasions, and it never failed to impress me. " We will require your assistance, and that of another able-bodied porter."

" Davies would be the man. He had B Company when I was A. And though A Company was always the smarter and better turned out, I have to admit that B was never far behind."

" Very good," said Holmes, obviously amused by the man's reminiscences. " Doctor Watson here and I, along with Mr. Pillstone, will be hidden in the passage here, or possibly behind that screen I see in the corner. We know the appearance of the men for whom we are looking. When we see them, you will hear three sharp blasts on this whistle here, and you must then shut the doors and prevent anyone from leaving the gallery. We will then come to assist you. Is that clear ? "

" Perfectly clear, sir, thank you. Shall I fetch Davies now, sir ? "

" Please do so. Do not look for us when you return with him. We will be concealed."

" Do you really intend to spend all day in that passage, Holmes ? " I asked.

" Either there, or behind that screen, as I said. Do not feel that both of you need be present with me at all times, however. Indeed, Mr. Pillstone, I would very much appreciate it if you could ensure that this display has as wide a publicity as it is possible for you and the Museum to manage in a short time."

" You really expect that our thieves will come today ? "

" I am convinced of it. I am sure that they are watching for any sign connected with the cameos, and the idea that we are exhibiting all thirteen cameos—be sure to mention the plural—will excite their curiosity, given that they are in possession of the other twelve. I know this for a fact," he added, in answer to Pillstone's questioning look. " It is now nearly half-past nine. I would suggest that you and Watson take turn and turn about at two-hour intervals. So you will relieve Watson at half-past eleven."

" I can guess that you have a plan, Mr. Holmes, but I am not convinced that I can see what it is."

" I, too, am somewhat confused," I admitted to Holmes, when Pillstone was out of earshot, and we had secreted ourselves in the passage, with the door ajar a fraction, allowing the one of us who stood before the other a clear view of the cabinet in which the cameos reposed. However, he made no answer to my comment, and disposed matters so that he would be in the position from where we could both best watch the doings in the gallery.

It had been a matter of some thirty minutes only when Holmes, who was watching avidly through the door, stiffened. " It is he ! " he hissed to me.

" To whom do you refer ? "

" Sir William Ferguson himself. The head serpent approaches, without his tail, but I do not think he will try any of his tricks just now. Aha ! He has seen the thirteen cameos, and he is going to inspect them. Yes, he has read the notice saying that we will replace them, and his face is as black as thunder. He is turning and— Down, Watson, down ! " He broke off his speech and dropped, crouching, to the floor. I followed his example, though I was unsure of the precise reason for his actions. " He was looking directly at this door," he said to me, " and it is best if our faces are not visible at the usual height where one would expect to see them." He peered, still crouching. " Now he is going out of the room, and no doubt he will summon his minions soon." I peered through the crack, and observed the back of the stout red-haired former Member of Parliament as he stalked out of the room.

" To what end ? "

" I originally believed that he only wanted to create confusion, but as a result of the events of the past few days, I am now convinced that he indeed has a buyer for the stolen goods. The price that these cameos could fetch would easily be sufficient to equip a small army. Such a force could be used to wage a civil war in the event that it were generally believed that Home Rule was to be declared."

" He would be prepared to fight against the Government, you mean ? "

" I fear that is the case, Watson. But mark this, that the gems lose most of their value without the central figure which currently reposes in the case. I fear he may be planning to steal the cameo once more. I do not mean that he personally will do so, but we can expect a visit from his bully-boys soon enough."

" In broad daylight ? "

" It is possible, but I think unlikely. I feel we may stand down from our posts now, but we must ensure that the Museum staff continue to stand guard."

So saying, he stepped from the passage, and I followed. " We have seen the man we want, Jennings," he told the grizzled ex-soldier. " I do not think he will return, but I am convinced that there should be at least two good men on duty here at all times until the public has left the building, and there should be a guard posted all night."

" If I may be permitted, sir, I would like to volunteer for the night duty," said Jennings.

" I, too," added Davies, speaking for the first time. " I can find two more men to cover this post for the rest of the day, and I and CSM Jennings will be happy to stand guard for the night. It won't be the first time we've spent all night waiting for the trouble to come and find us, will it, Charlie ? "

" Indeed it won't. And it will be a damned sight more comfortable, begging your pardon for the language, sir, than the times we spent on the African plains, waiting for lions and leopards to come out of the bush at us. A lot more exciting than standing here all day, as well," he added.

" Very good," said Holmes. " We will all meet again this evening then. I would find your replacements now, and allow yourselves to rest before the night's vigil."

Holmes and I made our way to Pillstone's office and informed him of the developments.

" We must capture these rogues red-handed," said Holmes. " We cannot move against them on suspicion alone."

" What do you require of me ? " asked Pillstone. " I must confess, this is somewhat outside my usual line of duty."

" You must ensure that we have permission to remain in the Museum and do what is needed to protect the remaining cameo, and those two porters who seem so admirably suited to the task are allowed to assist us tonight."

" They are two of our finest men, to be sure, and I am

delighted that they have been so public-spirited as to volunteer for this task."

" Excellent," said Holmes. " We will remain here until the evening, if that is convenient. One or the other of us will be visiting the gallery at intervals during the day to ensure there is nothing untoward occurring."

As Holmes had explained, he and I took it by turns to visit the gallery, by the normal routes, rather than through the passages, at frequent intervals. I was returning from one of these visits, when I caught a glimpse in the crowd of a face that seemed somehow familiar to me. In a few seconds, I had marked the man as one of those who had burst into our rooms in Baker-street and threatened me and Holmes. I looked at the man next to him, and marked him as the man whose arm I had wounded, as was obvious from the fact that he carried the injured limb in a sling across his chest.

I quickly ducked out of sight of the men behind a pillar, watching carefully until they had gone down the stairs. I inferred that they had been sent on a reconnaissance sortie by Sir William in order to spy out the gallery, in preparation for an assault later that day, or in the night. I thereupon hurried to Holmes and informed him of what I had just seen.

" That confirms my suspicions that they are about to attempt the reacquisition of the cameo," he said. " I do not think they will attempt it in broad daylight, but will probably attempt to commit the theft after the Museum has closed."

" How will they effect an entrance, do you think ? "

" I am sure that in a building this size there will be many unguarded entrances. Bear in mind that they have McCoy's experience and expertise available to them, and it is almost certain that he will be informing them of the weakest points of entry to the building."

SHERLOCK HOLMES ACCORDINGLY advised the new porters standing guard at the gallery that they should continue to maintain a greater than usual vigilance over the gallery, and to be prepared to raise the alarm instantly should they become aware of any suspicious activity.

" I do not feel that anything will occur during the daytime, but it is possible that Sir William's impatience will outweigh his natural caution in this matter," he told Pillstone and myself.

As it transpired, Holmes' predictions were proven correct, and the day passed without incident. As the time for the closing of the museum to the public approached, Holmes addressed us.

" Watson, you and I will stand watch in the passage leading to the gallery. Pillstone, those whom we are about to face are dangerous men, and I have no wish that you should expose yourself to peril. After all, Watson and I have faced many dangers together, and we have the combined forces of the brave Jennings and Davies at our backs. Your task will be to wait at a suitable location and listen, and to summon the Scotland Yard police in the event that you deem it necessary or if you receive such instructions from Watson or myself. I wish you to ask for Inspector Lestrade if he is available, otherwise for Inspector Athelney Jones. If neither of these two men is available, then for Inspector Gregson."

" I understand," answered the curator.

" Watson, you have your stick with you ? " asked Holmes. I confirmed this, and he continued, " Come, then, let us to the gallery. We will not take the passages, since we must instruct Jennings and Davies as to their duties."

When we reached the gallery where the cameos were being displayed, we discovered the two ex-soldiers already there. " I would advise you to place yourselves where you cannot be seen from the door," Holmes told them. " The success of this enterprise will largely depend on surprise, and we wish to give no advance warning that we are aware of their plans."

" Very good, sir," replied Jennings. " We had assumed the same as yourself, sir, as it happens."

" I am glad to see you are men of intelligence," Holmes assured him. " You will have no problem staying awake and waiting for developments ? "

" Certainly not, sir. We've both stood our share of night sentry duty, don't you fear."

" Excellent. Doctor Watson and I will be concealed in the passageway behind the door. Do you have a whistle ? "

" Yes, sir," both men answered in chorus.

" Good. Summon the Doctor and myself in the event of anything untoward. In the event that I discover the intruders before you—"

" —Don't you worry yourself about that, sir. We will spot them first, I am sure."

" To be sure you will," agreed Holmes, " but it is as well to be prepared for even the most unlikely of eventualities. Should the Doctor or I discover the intruders first, then we will signal for aid with the whistles."

"How many are you expecting, sir?" asked Davies.

"Three, possibly four, but no more."

"Very good, sir," the former soldier answered, and he and his companion turned on their heels to take up their positions.

"And now we must conceal ourselves," Holmes said to me, opening the door set into the wall. We entered the darkened passage. While during the day the passage was lit by light admitted through openings set high into the walls, which also facilitated the circulation of air and provided ventilation, at night, the amount of light in the passage was reduced to the extent that I could hardly make out the figure of Holmes, though I knew him to be little more than two feet away from me.

We had waited some two hours. The heating in the Museum had been turned off when the visitors left, and my fingers and toes were beginning to suffer from the cold. I had started to rub my hands together in order to maintain my circulation, when Holmes gripped my arm.

"Hark!" he hissed in my ear. "Do you not hear them?"

I strained my ears to catch the sound that Holmes' sensitive senses had detected first. "I do," I confirmed, in the same low tones that Holmes had used. "But I cannot make out the direction."

"Nor I," he confessed. "Listen closely."

The sound of soft muffled footsteps, mixed with a metallic clinking sound, grew louder. It was plain to me that the noise of boots on the hard floor had been noted by the intruders as a result of their reconnaissance earlier in the day, and they had therefore taken appropriate precautions. The source of the metallic sound was less obvious until the light of a lantern abruptly flashed out from behind us. The villains were using the very passage in which we were concealed in order to make their entrance !

Holmes and I appeared to grasp the situation at the same time, and we both whirled round to face the invaders, who were approaching fast. The light of the lantern made it difficult to identify their faces, but it became obvious that they had recognised us.

" Mr. Holmes," came a voice that I recognised. " How good of you to wait for us. Shall we finish the game that we started earlier ? "

" You would do well to learn the manner of opponent you face before you talk about playing games," retorted Holmes, withdrawing the whistle from his pocket, and uttering three sharp blasts. At the same time, I reached past Holmes and pushed open the door leading to the gallery. The moonlight shining through the windows came through the aperture, and we were able to see our opponents more clearly.

There were four of them—the three who had visited Baker-street, and a fourth in their rear, whom I did not instantly recognise, but soon identified as McCoy. It was now obvious to me how the ruffians had learned of the existence of the passages, and how they had navigated them successfully to reach the gallery.

As Holmes and I stepped out of the passage into the gallery itself, I heard the sound of two pairs of boots running towards us. Jennings and Davies had responded to the call of the whistle, and I felt easier in my mind that we were now evenly matched as regards numbers. The large man who had threatened me in Baker-street stepped forward and faced Holmes.

" You are not in a position to argue with us this time," he snarled. " This time, you will take the punishment you deserve, and take it like a man." With these last words, he swung his heavy stick at his opponent's head, but Holmes had sufficient time to duck down and avoid the blow, as the stick swished over his head, missing its mark by a matter of several inches. As he bent, I saw his hand dart to the pocket where I knew he carried the riding-crop. As he straightened, he darted forward inside his opponent's reach, and the whip end of the crop shot forward, catching the giant smartly on the wrist holding the stick.

Immediately, the stick tumbled to the ground, and the Irishman let out a strangled hiss. " You will die for that, Mr. Holmes, even if I swing for it," he rasped out.

" Don't be a fool, Harry," said the other. " The other one's got a gun, like as not, and will shoot you down if you try anything, like he did to me the other day."

" I said I'd swing if I had to. Swing or die from his bullets, it's all the same. No-one treats Harry McLeod that way and gets away with it."

" Don't do it, Harry," urged the third man. " You know what our job is. It's to get the statue or whatever you call it and to take it back. There'll be plenty of time in the future to settle scores with these two."

" There are two more of them," pointed out McCoy from the rear of the party. " I recognise you, Jennings and Davies. Now if you will stand aside, and you as well, Mr. Holmes and Doctor Watson, we can proceed with our business, and no-one will be hurt."

" Go to H____ ! " burst out the leader. " I'm in charge of you lot, and I say what happens here. And what's going to happen here is that Mr. Holmes is going to learn that it doesn't pay to annoy Harry McLeod."

" I would say, rather," said my friend in an affable tone, " that it is you, Mr. McLeod, who should learn both manners and prudence."

" Hark at him ! " mocked McLeod. " Brave little bantam, isn't he ? " He unleashed a left hook in the direction of Holmes' face, which would undoubtedly have felled him had it reached its target, but Holmes dodged it easily, as well as the straight right with the injured hand that followed.

" I can play this game all night," jeered McLeod. " Can you ? "

" Give over," pleaded the man with his arm in a sling. " Let's just do this b____ job and get out of here."

For answer, McLeod wheeled round and fetched a massive open-handed blow to the side of the speaker's head that knocked him off his feet. " Now will you all learn to shut your mouths ? " he asked. " Mr. Holmes, are you ready to receive what is coming to you ? "

" I am ready, but I am not yet convinced that you are prepared," retorted Holmes. With these words, he stepped forward, the riding crop once more flashing out, and catching McLeod across the eyes.

" You b____ ! You have blinded me ! " cried out the giant, staggering back and clapping his hands to his face as Holmes reversed the riding-crop and brought the weighted handle down once, twice, thrice, upon the man's head just behind the right ear. McLeod crumpled to the ground silently, as his two accomplices and McCoy looked on in what appeared to be a kind of petrified fear.

" That's it for you two," snapped out Jennings, and

he and Davies moved to secure the two ruffians, who had both by now dropped their sticks, while I moved to McCoy, and ordered him not to move. Holmes, standing beside the unconscious McLeod, blew his whistle once more. He was rewarded by the sound of footsteps, and Pillstone entered.

" Thank God you are safe," he exclaimed, once he had taken in the situation. " The police are on their way, and I have given instructions to the porters on duty at the front door to admit them and show them here immediately they arrive." He paused. " You have not killed him ? " he asked, looking at Holmes' victim.

" I have not," replied Holmes, " though if I had, it would have been justified as self-defence. I have sufficient witnesses to back my statement on that. Do you know who will head the police arriving here ? "

" I was not informed, I am sorry to say."

" No matter. We will take what Fate sends us," he answered phlegmatically. " Ah, I hear the tread of official feet, if I am not mistaken."

In less than a minute, half a dozen uniformed police, headed by Inspector Lestrade in plain clothes, entered the gallery.

" I might have guessed I would see you here," said the inspector, smiling. " You have some interesting company tonight. Harry McLeod," looking down at the recumbent figure at Holmes' feet. " We have been after him for some time. There is a substantial amount of plate that has gone missing from houses around London recently, and we are pretty certain that these losses are the results of his efforts. And here we have Hugh Johnstone and Ian Gordon, if I am not mistaken. Yes, a pretty little bunch of housebreakers, indeed. Much indebted to you, Mr. Holmes. And this one ? " gesturing towards my captive.

" This is Mr. McCoy, lately on the staff of this Museum," explained Holmes. " He will be joining the other three. However, I must warn you to be careful in your questioning of these men. There are issues at stake that could affect the security of the Realm."

" From any other man, I would take that as exaggeration, but from you, Mr. Holmes, I will take it as a statement of fact. Will you and the Doctor here be accompanying us to the station ? "

" No, I fear not, Lestrade. We have a call or two to make first."

" As you wish." The Scotland Yard detective gave orders that the four men be taken to the police station, and locked up for the night. " On what charges, Mr. Holmes ? "

" You may start with assault and illegal confinement, and in the case of this one," pointing towards McLeod, who was being dragged, stumbling, across the floor to the door, " of attempted murder, the intended victim being myself. Other charges may appear later, but I think these will do for now."

" Very good. We will require a statement from you and the Doctor in due course."

" I hope I will be able to bring you more than that, Inspector, when we come to call. I would remind you once more to keep this matter confidential."

We left the Museum, leaving the perplexed Pillstone to answer any further questions that Lestrade might see fit to ask.

" Where to now, Holmes ? " I asked.

" We are going to pay a call, but I do not expect

anyone to be at home," was the strange answer to my question. " Follow me." We took some strange turns through streets and alleys which were unknown to me, but seemed familiar to Holmes. At length, he stopped in a narrow road, bounded on each side by high buildings, exclaiming " This is the place."

" Where do you mean ? " I asked, looking at the warehouses around us.

" This is not our destination," he smiled. " This is the starting point of our journey. Be so kind as to hail a cab on the main street and bring it here."

I returned to the main road where I hailed a hansom, and ordered it to the place where I had left Holmes standing. He mounted, and we started in the general direction of the East End, Holmes giving directions to the jarvey through the trap in the roof as we drove along. I did not hear him provide any address at any point in our journey, with his instructions being restricted to " Left here," " Straight on for a hundred yards and then right," and directions of that nature. Eventually, he called a halt, and we paid off the cab.

" Wait here for us," said Holmes, slipping a sovereign into the man's hand. " If we have not returned in one hour, you are free to leave, but in that case I would ask you to give this to the nearest police station." He scribbled in his note-book, tore out the leaf, folded it and handed it to the driver. " Do you understand ? "

" I do."

" Good. Watson, follow me." We made our way down a stinking alley, with Holmes pausing and examining the door of every house on the left of us. At the fifth such door, he stopped.

" This is the place, Watson," he said, trying the door,

but finding it locked. " I had suspected as much," he remarked. With a deft movement, he extracted a jemmy from his coat pocket. " Hold the door to stop it from flying open while I force the lock," he instructed me. " Do not fear, this is in a good cause. The jury is sure to acquit you, Watson," he added, jocularly.

A few seconds' prying were all that was needed to burst the door open, and Holmes and I entered the darkened hallway. There was just enough light for us to see our way to the stairs, which Holmes mounted before entering the back room. The only furniture there was an iron bedstead without a mattress. A used unmentionable stood beside it. As we approached the bed, I noticed a pair of handcuffs, with one cuff secured to the frame, and the other, open, dangling free. Holmes approached the bed, and dropped to one knee, inserting the blade of his knife between two floorboards. He removed one of the boards with a grunt of satisfaction, and extracted a few sheets of paper from the cavity so revealed, thrusting them into his pocket. He then used another attachment of the knife on the handcuffs, removing them from the bed, and thrusting them into his jacket pocket.

" And now for the crowning glory of this abode," he announced, leading the way down the stairs. " That is, if my calculations in this matter are correct." We entered the back room, where Holmes went straight to the mean dresser standing by the wall. " Yes, they are still here, it would appear," he told me. " Take a look for yourself."

He reached to the top shelf of the dresser, and handed me a small wad of folded newspaper. It was somewhat heavier than I expected, and Holmes marked my surprise.

" Open it carefully," he advised me, " preferably over the kitchen table."

I followed these instructions, and was astounded to discover one of the cameos within the paper. Even in the dim light filtering through the dirty window, it was apparent to me that the workmanship was of the same quality as the one depicting Our Lord which Holmes had restored to the Museum.

" How did you know this was here ? " I asked Holmes, but he declined to give a response, instead passing me eleven more newspaper packages.

" Let us leave this place," he said, shuddering. " I do not wish to remain here longer than is absolutely necessary." It was not like my friend to take such a strong dislike to a place in this way, but I refrained from questioning him further, and engaged myself in placing the twelve Apostles into a basket which I discovered under the table.

" And now onward," Holmes urged me. Carrying the basket, I followed him out of the house to where the cab was still awaiting our return.

" The Savile Club," ordered Holmes. He glanced at his watch. " A quarter after eight. He should be there now."

" Who ? "

" Sir William Ferguson, of course."

During the course of our journey, Holmes undertook an extraordinary transformation, removing his collar and tie. Shrugging off his topcoat and cutaway, he doffed his waistcoat, replacing it with his cutaway alone, turning up the collar, and pulling down his hat to shield his face. " It will have to suffice," he remarked. Give me the basket with the cameos," he requested as we drew outside the Club and dismissed the cab. " I want you to wait there, Watson, out of sight, but in a position where you may see what is going on. Take my coat and be ready to lend your assistance, as it is quite possible that I will require it should events proceed adversely."

I concealed myself, as far as was possible, behind a pillar, from which I could observe Holmes as he talked to the porter, informing the latter in an accent resembling that of his earlier attacker that Harry McLeod wished to speak to Sir William Ferguson. On being informed that Sir William was at dinner, he emphasised the fact that he had the basket with him, and expressed his opinion that Sir William would be more than happy to see him and the basket. Eventually, the porter seemed to accept the entreaty, and left to summon Sir William, who arrived, obviously irritated at having had his meal interrupted, his napkin still tucked into his collar. He was red-faced, and a little unsteady on his feet, and I therefore judged him to be somewhat in liquor.

Holmes addressed him, with his face turned somewhat away.

" I've brought them here for safe-keeping," he said, maintaining the accent that he had used previously. " All thirteen of them."

" You fool ! " exploded Sir William in a loud booming voice. " Why could they not have been left where they were ? Where are the other men ? And where's McCoy ? "

" That nosey-parker Holmes was sniffing round too close," my friend told him. " We thought it best to split up and confuse him and that doctor friend of his. Don't you want to see what we prigged from the Museum just now ? " he invited, holding out the basket for Sir William's inspection.

" Oh, dash it all, if you really think it necessary for me to inspect it," sighed the other, reluctantly, extending his hand to receive the expected valuable. In a flash, one wrist was encircled in steel with the handcuffs that Holmes had concealed in the basket.

" And now the other hand," said Holmes, in his usual accents, suiting his action to the words, and snapping the other cuff around his wrist.

" This is monstrous," protested the other. " Help ! Pol— ! " The Club porter moved forward, but Holmes waved him back.

" This is official business," he informed the servant. To Sir William he added, " I scarcely think that calling for the police is altogether advisable in this instance, do you ? However, if you insist, let us visit the police together," bundling his prisoner into a cab.

" You have no right to do this ! This is illegal detention and abduction," snarled Sir William.

" Not so," answered Holmes. " This paper," producing it from his inside pocket, " signed by the Home Secretary himself, grants me the powers of a special constable in this case." At the sight of the document, Sir William visibly subsided and ceased to offer any resistance. " Watson, take these," commanded Holmes, handing the basket containing the cameos to me, " and follow us to Scotland Yard."

When I arrived, and Sir William Ferguson had been escorted to a cell, Holmes confronted Lestrade and myself, who had been joined by Pillstone from the Museum.

" These are yours, at least temporarily, I believe," he

said, presenting the basket containing the cameos to the puzzled curator.

Pillstone gingerly removed one of the cameos from its newspaper wrapping, and a delighted smile spread across his face. " How do I ever begin to thank you ? " he exclaimed. " All twelve are here ? " Holmes nodded silently, and Pillstone eagerly began to unwrap the remaining cameos, a look of delight on his face. " These will go on display in the next few days," he told us, " and the exhibit will include a note of thanks to you, Mr. Holmes, for your invaluable assistance in this matter."

" I would prefer it if my name were not mentioned. Believe me, this affair has been much more than a mere matter of theft."

" A mere matter of theft, do you say ? " cried Pillstone, incredulously. " These cameos are priceless, as I explained to you earlier. The theft, had it succeeded, would have ranked as one of the most daring and successful of its type in history."

" Nonetheless," answered Holmes, " the theft would have been of little consequence when compared with the other possible outcomes."

" I fail to understand you."

" It is probably best that you remain in ignorance regarding this matter, Mr. Pillstone. I mean no offence to you, but there are some things which are best left unknown."

We left the police station, and Holmes turned to me. " It is time, is it not, that you learned the whole history of this affair ? "

" I must confess that I am in the dark about many of the events surrounding this," I admitted.

" In that case, let us take dinner at Alberti's or some

other establishment of your choosing, and I will reveal all."

I assented readily, and within thirty minutes we were seated in a quiet corner of an excellent French restaurant in Soho which had been recommended to me by one of my patients. The food and wine were first-class, and Holmes and I were contentedly puffing on our cigars when he began to speak of the business that had just concluded.

"THIS WAS, IN MY OPINION," he began, " a case in which I have been at my most stupid and blundering."

" You can hardly lay that charge at your door," I retorted. " Surely, with all the thieves now safely behind bars, and the mastermind of the plot with them, you can congratulate yourself on a successful conclusion."

" Even so," Holmes said, " I was culpably negligent in my handling of the business, as you will hear. In the first place, in your opinion, Watson, who do you consider it was who stole the cameos and substituted those caricatures ? "

I was under the impression that this was some kind of test of my reasoning abilities, and therefore endeavoured to give as good an account of myself as possible. " I had my suspicions that it was McCoy—"

" Pah ! " expostulated Holmes. " Suspicions ? Surely it was obvious ? "

I ignored the outburst and continued, " —but I have little or no clue as to why he did it."

" Really ? I had expected more of you than that, Watson. I confess to being sadly disappointed in you."

Though the criticism stung, I managed to refrain from making a reply, and attempted to think charitably of Holmes.

" Surely you noticed the man's name ? " continued Holmes. " As well as his place of origin ? "

" What of them ? "

" McCoy is surely a name associated with the Protestants who live in the northern part of Ireland. This group is strongly opposed to Home Rule, as you are no doubt aware."

" This is true," I conceded.

" And the cameos came from the Vatican, which I have no doubt McCoy as a staunch Protestant would see as a nest of enemies, to be discomfited or worse."

" I agree that he might have some motive there. But the means, Holmes ? "

" You saw for yourself the secret passages by which it is possible to move silently and invisibly through the museum. We established, did we not, that McCoy was wearing slippers and stayed late on the night before Pillstone visited us ? That is, on the night that the cameos were stolen. You will remember that when we visited the gallery, the metal quarters of our shoes rang on the floor. Slippers would allow him to move silently through the gallery towards the cabinet."

" Would he not have required the key to the cabinet ? Pillstone kept that key in his possession all the time."

" He had no need of the key, Watson. Remember that I enquired of Pillstone regarding the replacement of the glass in the cabinet ? There was glazier's putty still soft between one of the glass panels and the wooden frame. Some of that putty had fallen to the floor, and it was that which I picked up and saved in the envelope. When you went out earlier today to purchase my tobacco, I placed some of the putty from the cabinet and the floor and examined it through the powerful microscope that stands on the table by the window. This was not a definite proof," he admitted, " but in my experience there are considerable differences between the different types of putty available on the market. There was another sample on the floor of the office beside McCoy's boots. When I examined this sample in its turn, although it would not constitute proof that McCoy was the thief, I would take my oath in Court that the samples of putty from the cabinet and from the office are from the same batch. This microscopic examination was really only necessary for my own peace of mind, as I was convinced that McCoy was guilty, and the mere existence of putty in two locations was sufficient to confirm my deduction that he had removed the glass and replaced it after having removed the cameos."

" The sample in the office might have been introduced after McCoy had first examined the cabinet with Pillstone, rather than at the time of the theft," I objected.

" You make a good counsel for the defence, Watson, but I consider it far more likely, in the absence of other evidence, that the putty was carried in on his slippers, once he had removed and replaced the pane of glass, and was deposited on the floor when he removed his slippers to change into his boots. The deed was obviously carried out after the floor of the gallery had been cleaned."

"You would find it hard to prove all of that in a court of law."

"Indeed, but there is more. When McCoy went to the gallery to prepare the way for us, while I was drinking the tea he had prepared, I examined his desk in as unobtrusive a manner as I could accomplish. On the desk I chanced to see a receipt from an ironmonger's in Camden. The items purchased by McCoy and listed there were a tin of glazier's putty, a glazier's palette knife, and a sheet of glass of the same dimensions as that in the cabinet. I assume that the latter was purchased as a precaution, should he chance to break the original in the course of removing it using the palette knife. As it happened, he did not appear to require it, since the cabinet glass seemed to be of the same composition as the other panes there."

"You appear to have at least determined the identity of the thief in a remarkably short pace of time," I remarked.

"I had also gained a little time to examine the office without McCoy's being present by upsetting the exhibit in the gallery, as you must have noticed. I am afraid that I let my triumph show in my eyes, and as we saw, McCoy slipped away from the Museum to join his colleagues in crime. As I mentioned before, it was clear to me that McCoy was not acting alone. I had already consulted brother Mycroft on the matter immediately after Pillstone had related the details of the theft, suspecting that there was more to the matter than mere theft, and he had informed me of the existence of Ferguson's group, immediately pointing out to me the political connections—an area in which Mycroft, as you know, is an expert. He had also furnished me with an appointment as a special constable, which you saw proved so useful to me when we finally came to settle matters with Sir William.

" As soon as McCoy had flown the coop, it was obvious to me that I had to locate the whole gang if the cameos were to be recovered. I had only one starting point to go on, and that was Sir William Ferguson. I therefore determined to watch his house, and was soon rewarded by the sight of McCoy paying a call. When he emerged ten minutes later, I was faced with a dilemma. Mycroft had impressed upon me the importance of keeping the whole business a secret, should Ferguson prove to be involved, as he now was. There was therefore no possibility of my involving the police. I had two choices, the first being to ransack Sir William's house and retrieve the cameos—a plan that would have to wait until nightfall were I to carry it out. The second was to follow McCoy and apprehend him before questioning him closely about the group with whom he was working, in an attempt to force Sir William's hand. This was the course I chose.

" Foolishly, I did not take sufficient precautions. Maybe the cold from which I was suffering prevented me from clear thought. In any event, I had just turned down a deserted side-street to follow McCoy when I was seized from behind, and a harsh voice spoke in my ear.

" 'You think that you are a clever man, Mr. Holmes," it said. 'Show us how clever you can be. Just keep quiet for a few days and no harm will come to you.' A foul gag was stuffed in my mouth, and some sort of bag was placed over my head, so I could not cry out for help, or see where I was. My arms were gripped tightly from behind, and in this condition I was forced into some sort of carriage. Happily, I had an exact knowledge of my location at the point that I had been taken, and I forced myself to remember every turn and movement of the cab."

" I remember that you had no address to give our driver earlier. You were remembering the route you had taken while blindfolded ? " Though I was well aware of Holmes' powers of memory and concentration, the feat of remembering the journey he had undertaken under such circumstances filled me with a certain wonder.

" We arrived at our destination," Holmes continued, " and I was bundled out of the cab, and into a house, where, the bag still over my head, I was marched up the stairs. Abruptly, the bag was removed from my head, and my hands were released. Immediately, I removed the gag from my mouth, and then beheld my captors. They were the same three that we have already encountered, and it was to their leader, whom we now know to be named Harry McLeod, that I addressed myself.

" 'I do not expect you to tell me your name, or that of your friends,' said I to him, 'but I would appreciate your letting me know how long I may expect to be your guest.'

" 'If all goes well, you will be free to work your mischief in a few days. It all depends on the generosity of another.'

" I was intrigued by this pronouncement, but forbore to enquire much further. It was clear to me that this man was the leader, and his countenance bore the look of a man with a little more intelligence than his fellows. If I were to find out more, it was not to my advantage to be questioning him.

" I had not much time to consider the matter, for my

left wrist was seized, and I was handcuffed to the bed that you saw in that room. 'Food and water will be provided,' my captor told me, and I was left alone to consider my fate.

" They had omitted to remove the contents of my pockets, and had I been carrying a revolver, or indeed, any kind of weapon, I could easily have escaped. As it was, with some difficulty I managed to extract a small slip of steel from my waistcoat pocket, and contrived to slip the pawl of the handcuffs. It is an easy trick to accomplish, provided one has the right tools. At this point I determined to hide the warrant giving me authority as a special constable. Such an official document would undoubtedly have tipped my hand as regards the value of the prize I knew to be at stake. This was among the papers I retrieved earlier from under the floor of the room where I had been held.

" After I had replaced the floorboards, I crept to the door of the room, and listened carefully. I did not anticipate that a sentry would be posted outside, and indeed, I could hear no sign of one. There was a confused sound of voices coming from down the stairs, but I could make out few of the words, and those I was able to distinguish appeared to be chiefly concerned with a dispute regarding who should go to buy beer for the group.

" After a short while I heard footsteps starting to ascend the stairs, and I returned to the bed, re-securing the handcuff about my wrist. I feigned sleep, until my gaoler, who was one of the smaller men who had appeared earlier.

" 'Here's your grub," he said to me, placing a piece of stale bread and a tin cup of water beside the bed.

" 'How long do you expect me to be here ? ' I asked, as pleasantly as I could manage, given the circumstances.

" 'When his nibs has got rid of the sparklers, or whatever you want to call them,' was the answer I heard. This news was exciting to me, as you can imagine. This gang of low-born ruffians was being controlled by someone else.

" 'Sir William Ferguson ? ' I asked. The Irishman's eyes grew narrow.

" 'Ask me no names and I'll tell you no lies,' was his only answer, by the tone of which I knew that I had scored a hit. I felt it inadvisable to pursue any further enquiries, so thanked him for the vile repast, and he left me. The bread was stale and the water foul, and I merely nibbled and sipped at them, following which I lay on the bare bedstead, and dozed. As you know, I am accustomed to some hardships from time to time in the course of my work, so this lack of sustenance was little more than an inconvenience that I hoped would be merely temporary. I had satisfied myself that I could set myself at liberty within the confines of the room, but I was unsure as to whether I could escape from the building where I was confined. The window of the room where I was being held captive had been boarded up, with only a small gap at the top to admit light, and it was impossible for me to remove the boarding—believe me, Watson, I attempted this—and equally impossible for me to see anything except a patch of sky, no matter from what angle I attempted to make my observations. I had, unfortunately, omitted to being with me my hand-mirror, which would have assisted me in this latter regard, but it was useless for me to reproach myself for this omission.

" At one point, I heard the front door of the house being opened, and the sound of a visitor being welcomed. The only visitor to the house of whom I could conceive was the man who had been referred to as 'his nibs' by my gaoler, Sir William Ferguson. I slipped out of the handcuffs, and listened with all my attention to the sounds coming from below. Happily, the visitor, whom I was now certain was Sir William, had a distinctive loud voice, as you probably remember from the incident outside the Club, and I was able to distinguish most of the words.

" 'Keep them wrapped up and keep them here,' came the voice. 'Old Engelhart will be along to see them in a few days.' The name was familiar to me as an American collector of art. I had heard once from Leverton, of the Pinkerton agency, that Engelhart was suspected of being the ultimate owner of the Rubens that disappeared from Applethorne House—a little before your time, I believe, Watson—but there was not enough proof to justify a warrant. At that moment, I knew that the theft of the cameos was not simply a matter of embarrassing the parties involved, but that there was a very large sum of money involved. This was confirmed by the next words I heard. 'And when that Yankee hands over the money, we'll have enough to put a gun in the hands of every mother's son who loves his country and hates Rome.' I knew then that I had to act to stop this transaction taking place. Once the money had been handed to Sir William, I knew that there would be little chance of its ever being retrieved."

" Sir William owned several banks and businesses on the Continent at one time, did he not ? " I asked.

" And as far as I am aware, he still does. Men such as

he have many ways of concealing large sums of money. Since Ferguson had mentioned that Engelhart might make his decision within the next few days, it seemed wise for me to move as soon as possible. I therefore determined to make my attempt at escape, with the cameos in my possession, some time early in the morning before dawn, when I judged that my guards' faculties would be at their lowest ebb. I made notes of all I had heard, and concealed them with the warrant, should they take it into their heads to search me at any time.

" I had left the house unarmed, and would have to rely on my fists should it become necessary to defend myself against any opposition. As you know, I have some skill in the noble art, and I felt confident, even were I to be faced with more than one opponent.

" When I judged the time to be just before dawn, I slipped out of the handcuffs and listened carefully. It took only a few seconds for me to realise that it was useless for me to make any attempt that night. At least two of my captors were awake and talking, with their conversation interspersed with snatches of drunken song. It was almost certain that if I tried to abstract the cameos, this would attract their attention, and while I might have been able to overpower two drunken men, there was no knowing how many others were in the house, who might be summoned to assist their comrades.

" I therefore returned to the bed and re-attached the handcuffs, sore at heart that I had been prevented from carrying out my plan. The next night was much the same—although I was ready to make my move, again I heard the sound of drunken roistering, and I judged it unwise to make any move."

" Were you being fed during this time ? " I asked Holmes.

" I was being given food of a kind, and water to drink. I cannot say that I was ill-treated, though it was far from luxury. In any event, Ferguson arrived at the house the next day, and again, his loud voice made its way up the stairs and through the door. I gathered that the cameos were to be sold the very next day.

" Accordingly, I determined that I should build up as much of my energy as was possible before making my attempt, though the cold from which I was suffering, which continued to worsen, was undeniably sapping me of much of my strength. I therefore determined to eat the food that was brought to me, however unpalatable it might be, but to my surprise it transpired to be an eminently passable Irish stew, brought to me by the same turnkey as before.

" He said nothing as he set the bowl before me, with a wooden spoon in it. 'Eat it,' he told me, not unkindly. 'You look as though you need it.' It was a human gesture from the man, and I returned it with my polite thanks. Believe me, Watson, it would be a mistake to mark down all these men as rogues and ruffians. Many of them are no more than discontents who feel they have been deprived of what they regard as their rightful due, and wish to put right what they regard as wrongs.

" My words and attitude had obviously had some effect on him, and he spoke to me. 'You'll be out of here soon enough. His nibs is going to be selling the goods tomorrow, and then you can go back to where you came from.' I expressed my gratitude, and he left me, realising that it was essential for me to make an attempt that very night, no matter what obstacles would present themselves, or whatever might befall me.

" I attempted to pick the lock of the door, having first listened to ensure that there was no sentry outside, and there were no sounds of the carousing I had heard on the previous nights. I was not expecting to encounter a guard, but one can never be too careful under such circumstances. The lock yielded easily and swiftly to the shim that I had used to slip the handcuffs, when employed as a picklock, and I made my way down the stairs taking are to make as little noise as possible."

" How did you know where the cameos were being kept ? " I could not refrain from asking.

" Ah, there you have most astutely put your finger on the spot," he told me. " For all I knew, the cameos were being stored under the pillow of the sleeping leader of the gang, in which case I would have no chance of abstracting them. In the event, I discovered them in the same place where we discovered them earlier this evening, but to my dismay, I had only removed and pocketed the first of them, which was in a place of its own, as befitted its subject, when I heard the noise of voices from the next room. It is quite possible that the newspaper in which the cameo was wrapped rustled when I placed it in my pocket, and disturbed a light sleeper in the next room. At any event, the room was suddenly illuminated by a lantern, and the leader of the gang stood before me, a heavy cudgel in one hand.

" I ensured that the cameo was safely stowed in my pocket, and prepared myself to meet him, snatching up one of the kitchen chairs as I did so. The cudgel swung at me, and I used the chair to deflect, but not entirely to break, the blow, which landed on my forehead, stunning me a little. I staggered, but managed to retain enough presence of mind to catch hold of the stick and twist it out of his hand. He dropped it with a grunt, and swung a left at me which I dodged easily, following it up with straight jab of my own which caught him in the right eye. Though I would have considered that this put him hors de combat, he continued to come at me, but this time I was able to intercept his fist with the chair, and he fell back, nursing his hand, which had obviously been injured by the blow.

" I was then able to follow up with a blow to his abdomen—hardly Queensbury Rules, I fear, but then he had already breached those by coming at me with a cudgel. Between that, the blow to his face, and the pain in his hand, he was temporarily out of action. One of his henchmen, the one who was not holding the lantern, came at me next, but I sprang to one side, finding myself against the back door of the house, which to my surprise I discovered to be unlocked and open as I felt the catch behind me click open in answer to the pressure of my weight against it. I had no idea where it would lead, but I felt instinctively that I would be better in the open air. Accordingly, I slipped through the door, my latest opponent hot on my heels. As I reached the outside, I saw his hand emerge through the doorway brandishing a knife. I quickly slammed the door, trapping the arm between the door and the frame, which resulted in the arm being quickly withdrawn and a shriek of pain from the other side.

" I found myself in a narrow alley between the backs of two rows of houses. The stench was vile, and the ground under my feet was slippery and filthy. At this point, I realised, to my intense chagrin, that I had left behind the warrant and the papers I had concealed earlier and I cursed myself silently as a fool. I was unsure of my precise location, but knew the house was in the East End of London. Naturally, there was no light, and the dawn was just breaking, so it was impossible for me to see any landmarks, but by great good fortune, as I ran around the corner into the street, I collided with a police constable on his beat, and we both fell to the ground.

" I wonder you were not arrested," I remarked, laughing despite myself.

" It was a close thing," he answered. " As you no doubt remarked when I returned here, my appearance was somewhat unprepossessing, and I was in somewhat suspicious circumstances. My manner of speech seemed to convince him that I was not of the class of common criminals, but I was still invited, in the strongest possible manner, to accompany him to the nearest police station. There, a piece of good fortune awaited me. The sergeant to whom I was handed was Urquhart, whom you may remember as a junior constable in connection with the Bishopsgate jewel case. He recognised me, despite my tattered and dishevelled appearance. Naturally, when I was searched, the cameo came to light, but my reputation with the sergeant saved me from an appearance in the magistrates' court.

" I discovered my exact location, and was able to hail a cab, whose driver seemed reluctant to take such a shabby-looking fare until our friend Urquhart persuaded him of my bona fides. I was mightily relieved, Watson, to see you here when I staggered through the door."

" It must have been quite an ordeal."

" It was most certainly an experience I am not anxious

to repeat," he laughed. " And at the same time, the whole affair has been a most salutary lesson to me."

" In what way ? "

" In that I bungled the case almost from the start. I knew McCoy was the guilty party almost from the beginning, and I should have treated the case as one of simple theft, and called in the police, rather than allowing brother Mycroft to persuade me that this was a melodrama which required such secrecy in its handling. When I visited him before going to the Museum for the first time, and he offered me the warrant authorising me as a special constable, I should have refused, and simply offered my detective powers, rather than acting as an enforcer of the laws. Hubris, Watson, sheer hubris," he sighed.

It was unlike Holmes to castigate himself in this way, but I could not help but agree with him, remarking inwardly to myself that the cold from which he had been suffering might be in some way to blame for his lapse of judgement in this regard.

McCoy and the three Irishmen who had attacked and confined Holmes and broken into the Museum were arrested and charged with assault and related charges. The cameos were never mentioned in court. Sir William Ferguson's decision to emigrate to Canada was widely reported in the Press, and though various reasons were hinted at, none came close to the truth.

Though Holmes' role in the affair of the Vatican cameos was never made public, he received the grateful thanks of the Cabinet for his work. In addition, though he never spoke of this afterwards, he was summoned privately to Ambrosden Avenue to receive the gratitude, accompanied by a small financial reward, of the Vatican, expressed through the person of the Archbishop of Westminster.

The Reigate Poisoning Case

Editor's Notes

This case confused me completely when I came across it in the box, with the handwritten sheets pinned together, in an unmarked manila envelope. In The Hound of the Baskervilles, *Watson refers to Holmes' actions where " he had defended the unfortunate Mme. Montpensier from the charge of murder which hung over her in connection with the death of her step-daughter, Mlle. Carère, the young lady who, as it will be remembered, was found six months later alive and married in New York".*

The case described here deals with a Mme. Montpensier who is associated with the murder of a step-daughter. However, in this case, though the name matches and the initial circumstances are similar, there is no mention of the daughter's survival or emigration to the United States of America.

One can only assume that this adventure here is a completely different case to that described in " Hound". Surely Watson could not have confused the two cases ? And yet we know that he did indeed relate strange discrepancies in his accounts of his famous friend's cases, well known and familiar to all who study the work of the great detective.

In this instance, we must assume that bonus dormitat Homerus *(" great Homer nods"), and that a half-remembered name associated with the New York case has somehow found itself attached as a pseudonym to the case I have here named the " Reigate poisoning case", similar to the Camberwell case as mentioned in the* Five Orange Pips.

In any event, the adventure is one in which Holmes'

scientific deductive talents are matched by a quality that cannot strictly be called " logic", but must be classified as " intuition". His final reasons for determining the guilt and innocence of the parties involved depend more on an understanding of human nature than they do on his forensic analytic skills. This is a new, and rather attractive, side to Sherlock Holmes that we see here.

※※※※※

M Y FRIEND, the consulting detective Sherlock Holmes, was possessed of strange moods and humours. I feared the times when no cases that demanded his full attention came to our door, for it was at those times that he turned to self-poisoning through his use—or I should rather say his abuse—of cocaine and morphine, and though I had largely cured him of these habits which threatened his reputation and career, I was all too aware of the possibility of a relapse.

It was with some relief, therefore, that I heard Madame Montpensier confide her troubles to him, for the case promised, on first hearing, to be one of those where Holmes' talents and capabilities were to be stretched to the fullest, thereby occupying his mind, and removing the temptation of the hypodermic syringe as a distraction. Nor were these initial impressions mistaken, as events were to show us.

The lamps along Baker-street were being lit when our client was ushered into our room. She was of an indeterminate age, possibly about forty-five years of age, and undoubtedly had been an exceedingly handsome woman in her prime, but time and experience had laid their gentle hands on her. Her presence brought a breath of sophisticated femininity to the somewhat barbaric masculine atmosphere of our rooms, and Holmes himself appeared not to be insensible of the fact as he waved her to a chair.

" Please be seated, madam," he invited. " How may we help you ? "

She answered in a voice that bore slight traces of a foreign accent. " My name, as you saw on the card that I sent up, is Louise Montpensier. I am a widow, but have remarried, and until two days ago, I lived with my step-daughter, the child of my first husband, in our house in Reigate."

" There has been some change in the circumstances ? " enquired Holmes.

" Indeed there has," she replied. " My beloved Annabel is dead. She died recently—all too recently—and it was I who was responsible for her death, but I swear to you that I am no murderer ! " Following this outburst, she broke into a fit of hysterical weeping, which lasted for some minutes. From past experience, I knew there was little relief that I as a doctor was able to bring to her, other than dashing a glass of water in her face, or taking some similar form of drastic action, which I was understandably unwilling to do under the circumstances.

While she was in this condition, Holmes glanced at me, and shook his head slowly, but I was unable to determine the exact meaning of his action. At length, the sobs died down, and our visitor produced a handkerchief with which she proceeded to wipe her eyes.

I offered her a drink of water, which she accepted with

thanks, and it was this that she sipped while proceeding to tell us her story.

" First of all, Mr. Holmes, I want you to know before others inform you of the fact, that I have lived a life of which some might disapprove. I came from Belgium when I was sixteen years old, as a singer and dancer. Without any vanity, I can tell you that I displayed an uncommon gift for these arts, and was blessed with looks that attracted a number of men. But such a life does not last for ever, and as my voice and my looks faded, I cast around for some anchor with which I might moor the barque of my life, if I may be permitted such a metaphor.

" I found such a man in Richard Stevens. He was a widower of some fifty years of age, and though he had full knowledge of my past and of my reputation, he loved me truly. He was such a man as I had long hoped for—true in heart, and steadfast in his love. He had one daughter from his previous marriage, who was then ten years of age, and Annabel and I were like mother and daughter from the day we first set eyes on each other. I can truly say that the six years during which I was married to Richard Stevens were the happiest years of my life. He never gave me any cause for complaint, and I can swear to you that the same was true of me. I loved that man with all my heart, Mr. Holmes, and would have done anything to avoid giving him pain.

" As for Annabel, his daughter, she was a delight to me. I had long ago resigned myself to the fact that I am unable to bear children of my own, and so all the love I would have expended on my own child was poured on Annabel, and she responded in kind. I watched her grow from a young girl into a young woman whose beauty, I could see, exceeded my own at the height of my fame. But was I jealous ? No, I was not," answering her own question. " I was delighted that the child of my beloved Richard was of such a unique and distinctive nature."

" Can you tell us anything of her mother ? " asked Holmes.

" I have seen her portrait, which was of a delicate, somewhat sickly-looking young woman. She had apparently died while giving birth to her second child, which was stillborn. At that time, Annabel was three years of age, and therefore she has—had, I should say—little or no knowledge of her mother. She had been brought up by a series of nurses and governesses until my marriage to Richard Stevens.

" But our Eden was shattered. It was the night before Christmas three years ago. My Richard had been buying gifts for us—Annabel and myself—and was returning home. It was a cold night, and the snow had fallen heavily in the streets, but had melted in the daytime and had re-frozen. He slipped on the ice, and on account of the weight of the parcels he was carrying, lost his balance and fell under the hoofs of the horses drawing an omnibus. His mangled body was brought home to us." Her voice trembled as she told us this sad tale, and her handkerchief went to her face.

" A terrible accident," I sympathised.

" Indeed," agreed Holmes. " May I be impertinent and ask how his death affected you financially ? "

" He was a rich man," she answered. " His will provided for Annabel and myself at least adequately. The house, and all in it, was made over to me, as well as sufficient money for us to continue our lives in the accustomed style. The bulk of his money was to be held in trust, to be presented to Annabel upon her marriage, or when she reached the age of twenty-one, whichever was the sooner."

" And should your step-daughter die before either of those events ? "

" In such circumstances, the will dictated that I should be the beneficiary."

" And is there a considerable sum of money involved ? "

" More than considerable, I would say. Somewhere in the region of six hundred thousand pounds."

" Dear me," remarked my friend. " That is indeed a substantial sum. You mentioned that Mr. Stevens was your first husband, though. You have married again ? "

" I have, and I wish I had never done so," replied our visitor, with some show of indignation. " Mr. Ferdinand Colethorpe has proved the worst of husbands, as my Richard was the best, and yet, by the damnable laws of England, I am unable to divorce him, much as I wish to do so. I feel so little attachment to him that I have ceased to use his name, and have reverted to the name under which I entered this world—that is to say, Montpensier, though with my advancing years, I feel that ' Madame' rather than " Mademoiselle' is an appropriate form of address."

" Your husband treats you cruelly ? " I enquired.

" No, he does not. I almost wish to God that he did, for it would at least show that he recognised my existence. No, he ignores me completely. He leaves the house for months at a time, then suddenly re-appears. I have no advance knowledge of his comings and goings. One day he is here, and the next—*pouf* ! " She spread her hands. " And then it may be two months later, or even three, that I come down to breakfast and he is sitting at the table. And what does he say to me ? I will tell you. Nothing ! " Her bosom heaved, her Gallic temperament seemingly roused at the memory of her husband, and it took a little time before she appeared to be composed enough to continue.

" We will return to Mr. Colethorpe in good time," remarked Holmes. " But you told us that your daughter—your step-daughter, that is—is dead by your hand. How and when did that happen ? "

" It was just two days ago," our fair guest told us. " I went to her bed-room in the morning, as was our custom. I used to sit on her bed and we would talk about the day that had just passed, and the day to come, and—I may simply tell you that we had no secrets from each other. That fateful day, I entered her chamber and she appeared to be asleep, which was unusual. I shook her by the shoulder, but, my God, she was cold ! Cold as ice ! I put my ear to her nostrils to determine if I could detect any sign of life, but there was no breath in her body. I confess to you, Mr. Holmes, that I lost my head. I screamed, and the servants came running. At that point I must have fainted, for the next I knew was that I was in my own bed, with my maid beside me, bathing my temples.

" She informed me that the doctor had been called, and that he had pronounced my dear Annabel to be deceased, but without having been able to ascertain the cause of death. But I know it was I who gave her the fatal drink that caused her death."

" Indeed ? "

" Yes, it was I who gave her the last drink to pass

her lips. A cup of cocoa which she drank the previous evening before retiring. She was poisoned, I am sure of it, but I swear to you it was not I who introduced the fatal dose ! "

" Did the doctor give any indication of when the death might have occurred ? " Holmes queried.

" He judged that it might have happened any time after midnight. He is a fool. He says he has no idea of the cause of death."

" That takes us very little further forward. But the doctor tells you that the cause of death is still unknown. Why do you say poison ? "

" There were no visible marks of violence on the body. What can it be but poison ? There will be a post-mortem examination conducted tomorrow, they tell me. It is too terrible to think of." Once again, she buried her face in her handkerchief, seemingly overcome by grief.

" And you wish me to discover how she died ? "

" I do not wish you to tell me how she died, but you must determine whom it was who killed her ! It was murder, I tell you. Murder ! "

The last words were pronounced in an almost hysterical shriek, and I feared that the good Mrs. Hudson, accustomed as she was to Holmes' eccentricities, and those of his clients, would nonetheless be alarmed at the words and the tone of voice in which they were uttered.

" What makes you say this, Madame ? " asked Holmes calmly.

" It is Colethorpe at his tricks, I am sure of it. He has poisoned her."

" You are making a very serious accusation without any proof," remarked Holmes. " I fail to see where I can be of use, though, should the autopsy fail to reveal anything that substantiates your words."

" But do you not see ? " the wretched woman appealed to Holmes. " If the examination should discover any sign of foul play, it is I who will be suspected, since I am the gainer under the terms of the will and it was I who administered the fatal dose."

" Indeed," said Holmes, " but it is not my business to invent crimes where none exist. Apart from your justifiable distaste for a boorish husband, what reason do you have for believing that your step-daughter was murdered ? "

" A piece of paper bearing these words was discovered on her dressing-table," she responded, producing from her reticule a folded piece of notepaper, which she extended to Holmes. " This is a copy that I made in my own hand."

" Take it, Watson, and read it," he commanded me.

I did as I had been bidden, and began. " ' I write this in haste, and I am in fear of my future. I have seen him again at my window. The drink tonight tasted bitter in my mouth. I am afraid to sleep, because I know he will come tonight.' "

" The original was in your step-daughter's handwriting ? " Holmes asked, and receiving a nod in reply, continued. " The outpourings of a frightened soul, indeed. When was this note found, and by whom ? "

" As I said, this was written on a scrap of paper discovered on her dressing-table. It was found by my maid when the body was moved."

" Had she ever mentioned anything of which she writes here to you ? "

" No, never."

" This came as a complete surprise to you, then ? "

" Indeed."

" And the ' he ' who is mentioned here, you take to be your husband ? "

" Who else could it be ? " was her response, uttered in tones of some surprise.

" Who indeed ? " mused Holmes. " Did your step-daughter have admirers ? "

" Naturally she did, but I knew of none who would have dreamed of such an act as visiting her at night in such a fashion."

" Let us return to Mr. Colethorpe. When did you last see him ? "

" Over a month ago. He suddenly appeared in the house one morning, as is his fashion, and stayed, speaking to no-one except the servants, for three days before leaving."

" And you have had no communication with him since that time ? "

Our guest gave a rueful smile. " You do not know the man, Mr. Holmes, or you would not waste your time asking such a question."

" What were his relations with your step-daughter during the times when he was in the house ? "

" They were the same as his relations to me, and may best be described as complete indifference."

" Your case intrigues me, somewhat, Madame, but I feel unable to take the case unless the autopsy and the coroner's jury deliver a verdict that hints at foul play."

" I beg of you, Mr. Holmes. Even if the English law finds nothing untoward, surely you wish to see justice prevail."

"Very well," sighed Holmes. " Please give me your address, and the name of the doctor who was called."

She provided an address in Reigate, and the name of a medical practitioner, at which I started.

" Would Dr. Clifford's Christian name be Henry, by any chance ? " I asked. " And is he about my age, very tall and slim, with fair hair ? And a habit of stooping down when he addresses you ? "

" Yes, he corresponds to that description, and I believe his name is Henry. I take it you are acquainted with him ? "

" I am indeed. He was a fellow student at Barts, and I have memories of us walking the wards together."

" Capital," exclaimed Holmes. " Watson, I rely on you to revive those memories of student days in Dr. Clifford's mind when you visit him, and ask questions on my behalf. If you can prevail on him to allow you to attend the procedure tomorrow, thereby allowing you to make a report to me on the matter, that would be of great value."

" Thank you, Mr. Holmes, and you too, Dr. Watson." She rose to go, and I escorted her to the door. " You will let me know of any developments as they occur ? " she beseeched Holmes.

" Believe me, Madame, I will treat this case as I treat all cases that I take up—with all the skill and diligence at my disposal for as long as it continues to present interesting aspects. My fees will be at the usual scale. A very good day to you."

She seemed somewhat nonplussed by this rather curt dismissal, but gathered up her things and left, bidding us both a farewell.

The Reigate Poisoning Case

WHEN THE DOOR HAD CLOSED behind her, Holmes turned his penetrating gaze on me.

" Describe our visitor," he requested.

" I feel she described herself adequately," I replied. " A former demi-mondaine, who has achieved a certain measure of respectability through marriage. But I am puzzled by her attitude. Why does she protest her innocence in that way when no accusation has been made against her, even if the cause of death is determined to be poison."

" Indeed so. ' The lady doth protest too much,' do you not agree ? Of course she claims to have served the drink that caused her step-daughter's death. There is always something strange about such a client, and it invariably puts me on my guard. I will throw up the case should the evidence conspire to point to her as a guilty party. It is of benefit to neither my conscience nor my reputation to serve a client whose guilt is beyond doubt."

" But there is still doubt, you feel ? " I confess that my question was based somewhat on a prejudice in favour of our recent guest, whose appearance and general demeanour had impressed me favourably.

Holmes laughed. " My dear fellow, naturally there is doubt. We know almost nothing about the facts of the case other than those of which we were informed just now. Naturally my suspicions are aroused by the denial of a crime of which the denier has yet to be accused. Indeed, we have yet to determine whether there has been a crime at all. All we know at present is that there has been a sudden death, and there is to be an autopsy. These two things may, but do not invariably, spell murder."

" There is a certain mystery that attaches to the errant Mr. Colethorpe, though, is there not ? "

" I hardly see this as a mystery," laughed Holmes, but he failed to offer any further explanation, and I forbore to press him on the subject.

I continued, " By the terms of the will as it was drawn up, the estate would pass to Mme. Montpensier should the step-daughter die, which would mean that he would be in effective possession of a very large sum of money indeed. Does this not seem of any significance in determining his guilt ? "

" I feel that you underestimate our client's strength of mind, Watson. Perhaps you failed to notice the shape of her chin, and the set of her jaw, signifying a forcefulness and decisive nature that is not common in the sex, but when present, is present in full force, greater than that which obtains in the male of the species. I have my doubts as to whether her husband would be able to control her purse, no matter what promises may have been made at one time to love, honour and obey. No doubt you also failed to mark the fact that she plays the viola."

" How on earth– ? "

" Simple enough, my dear man. The mark on the collar of the plush dress where the instrument rests, the peculiar configuration of the fingertips of the left hand, and the difference between the length of the nails on that hand and those of the right make it obvious that either the violin or viola is her instrument, which she plays regularly, given the rosin dust from the bow which I observed on her left shoulder. Possibly she regards this as some consolation for the neglect from which she currently suffers. From the size of her hands, the viola seems more likely, but I could be mistaken. In any case, to return to your original question, I feel that Mr. Colethorpe would find it hard work to lay his hands on that money."

" But surely, that paper discovered by the servant points to his guilt ? "

" It points to no such thing. You are making an assumption that the ' he' mentioned in that document is Colethorpe, simply because our client has told us this, and you were sufficiently impressed by her suggestion to believe it, at least as a possibility. I have more than a suspicion that our client's personal financial circumstances may not be as comfortable as she led us to believe."

" What makes you say that ? "

For answer, my friend picked up a pair of gold pince-nez lying in their case on the table. " I expect a return visit soon, when our fair visitor realises that she has left them here. In the meantime, what can you make of her from examining these ? "

I took the proffered spectacles and proceeded to scrutinise them. " Remarkably little, I confess. They are of good quality, but a little worn." I handed them back to Holmes.

" They are indeed of excellent quality. The name of the opticians inside the case is that of the finest such business operating in Bond Street. The date on which they were sold, as we can see from the label affixed within the case, is more than three years ago, which we have been told was prior to the demise of the estimable Mr. Stevens. Therefore we may conclude that they were purchased using his money while he was alive. They are, as you so rightly remark, of the finest manufacture.

However, the case is much worn and scuffed, and has on its surface significant traces of candle wax."

" And what can you conclude from that ? "

" Two or three major points. Firstly, that these spectacles are used frequently, and that therefore the eyesight of Madame Montpensier is perhaps not as perfect as she would like. Maybe she is significantly older than the age she would have us believe. The lenses are quite strong, which indicates that her eyesight, at least when she views objects close at hand, is somewhat less than perfect. Next, that as the case is likewise of good quality, but the lacquer has been adversely affected by the candle wax, and has not been replaced or even cleaned in a proper manner, there is a lack of money for such purposes. The fact that one of the cork nose-pieces has become detached and has not been replaced also tends to strengthen this theory. I would guess that Mr. Stevens' will, pending the transfer of the principal, is in some way entailed so that the income goes towards the maintenance of the house, rather than towards the direct comfort of its inhabitants. Incidentally, we may also conclude that vanity prevents Mme. Montpensier from wearing these eyeglasses in public, since the exterior of the case is in such poor condition, and I cannot believe that a woman who pays so much attention to matters of dress would wish to appear with such an object exposed to public view."

" Remarkable ! " I exclaimed.

" Elementary," he replied. " It is simply a matter of drawing logical conclusions from the details that most people, such as yourself, see, but fail to observe the significance."

" Then whom do you believe is guilty of killing the

step-daughter ? " I enquired, impressed, as always, with Holmes' deductive powers.

" I have yet insufficient data to make any such pronouncement. We must visit the place and see the lie of the land for ourselves before casting such aspersions. First, I wish you to re-acquaint yourself with your old friend. Return when you have learned what there is to learn from the doubtless admirable Dr. Clifford, the colleague of your student days, although our client seems to think little of him, and let me know what you can discover. If, by some chance, you find yourself in a position to visit the mortuary and examine the body yourself at the autopsy, I will remind you once more that this would be of great value to me."

I HAD FOUND NO DIFFICULTY in locating Clifford's address from the medical directory before I left London the next day, and on ringing the bell and sending in my card, I was admitted instantly.

" Upon my word, Watson, it is good to see you. I had heard that you had been out East with the Army and had been wounded." My erstwhile friend had changed little since the days when we assisted each other in the dissecting-rooms at Barts, and he greeted me with enthusiasm.

" That is precisely the case," I confirmed, and proceeded to tell him a little about my adventures in Afghanistan. " However, I should tell you that I am here today at the request of Mr. Sherlock Holmes, of whom you may have heard."

" Naturally I have heard of him, but I must confess that I had not thought to associate you with the chronicler of his adventures. What is your particular interest ? "

" It concerns a death for which you signed the certificate only a few days ago. A Miss Annabel Stevens."

" Ah, yes. Naturally I remember the case. The poor girl had apparently died in the night from some unknown cause. A seizure or some such, but I could not be sure."

" There was no sign of violence, then ? "

" I was unable to detect any such. Indeed, there was no cause of death that I could ascertain. Has your friend attached some suspicion to the death ? Does he suspect foul play ? "

" That is what we wish to establish. You say there was no apparent cause of death that you observed ? "

" As I said, there was none that I could see. The autopsy will no doubt reveal more."

" Who is conducting the procedure ? "

" Our old anatomy professor, Dr. Menzies."

" Old Menzies," I laughed. " I can hardly believe he is still in harness."

" As fit and healthy as ever, and as much of a terror to his students as he was in our day."

" I take it you will be attending ? May I request that I might also be present ? "

" I will be attending, and I am sure there would be no objection to your presence. As it happens, you are just in time. It is scheduled for four this afternoon. Would you care to stay for luncheon ? "

I accepted his invitation, and we spent the meal reminiscing about old days, and my recounting tales of my service in India and Afghanistan, and some of the medical details connected with the cases of Sherlock Holmes with which I had been involved. Clifford showed little or no interest in the legal or criminal aspects of these adventures, but displayed a keen interest in the medical consequences of the crimes whose circumstances I related.

" I become tired of the living patients," he confessed. " They bore me and exhaust me. I have a fancy to turn to pathology as my specialty, and so this autopsy is another opportunity for me to approach Menzies with my thoughts on the matter."

" Each to his own," I laughed. " Post-mortem examinations have never been my favourite form of medical practice."

Clifford examined his watch. " Let us set off."

The autopsy revealed few clues to be revealed from an examination of the surface of the body. There were no marks of violence or of any type of assault. Menzies grunted as he reached for the scalpel.

" If I may ? " I said to him, as I reached towards the face of the young girl, silent in death, but still exhibiting traces of a rare beauty, as Mme. Montpensier had told us.

He nodded his assent. " It would seem that you have had some interesting experiences since I taught you last, Watson," he remarked sardonically. " Let us pray that your skills in the field of anatomy have improved somewhat since that time."

I ignored this rebuke to my professional abilities, having become inured to Menzies' constant criticism during my time as a student, and pried open one of the eyelids of the dead girl. A glance was enough to show me that the eyeball had rolled upwards, and the little of the iris visible showed me that the pupil was considerably dilated. Lifting the other eyelid revealed a similar symptom.

" Well, well, Watson," remarked my former professor. " Was this a lucky chance, or had you some reason for suspecting such an outcome to your actions ? "

" I had remarked the curled state of the fingers and toes, which seem to me to indicate that she had ingested some toxic substance."

Menzies lifted his eyebrows. " Your association with Mr. Holmes seems to have stood you in good stead," he commented. " Congratulations, Watson. Clifford, you failed to observe these signs ? I cannot think how you ever came to pass your final examinations." The sting of his former professor's rebuke obviously found its mark, as Clifford flushed slightly and lowered his eyes. " In any case," Menzies continued, " I think we may safely proceed straight to the stomach, gentlemen, thanks to Watson's intervention." So saying, he pulled down the sheet covering the torso, and moved the scalpel in a straight line down from the sternum.

About thirty minutes later, the body was decently covered once more, and Menzies turned towards Clifford and me. " We will have to postpone the inquest until such time as we receive the results of the analysis of the contents of the stomach, but I would concur with your preliminary deduction, Watson. This does indeed appear to be a case of poisoning. Well done." From a man who was usually miserly in the extreme when it came to giving praise, this was indeed a compliment. " Do you or Mr. Holmes have any interest in the matter ? " he enquired of me, regarding me sharply.

" Without wishing to provide details, I can tell you that such is the case."

" Hmph. Then I will not enquire further. I am sure that your friend has his code of professional conduct as do we doctors."

After the exchange of a few pleasantries, I took my leave of Menzies and Clifford, and caught the next train back to London. Holmes professed himself delighted when I returned to Baker-Street and told him of the events of the post-mortem. " So you suspect poison ? " he asked me.

" I see no alternative explanation of the state of the body," I answered him. " As to the type of poison, I have little idea at present. As Menzies remarked, this will no doubt be revealed at the inquest following analysis of the samples that were taken."

" The question to which I and Mme. Montpensier will most urgently need an answer is that of how the poison entered the body."

" You have been in contact with her again ? "

" As we expected, she returned for her pince-nez, and stayed to talk a little more, with somewhat more candour on this occasion. Her hysteria appeared to have abated somewhat, and I may pride myself on having created a pleasant social atmosphere in which we could converse. As we suspected, she is not as well-off as she originally led us to believe, though she is far from being destitute. She will undoubtedly benefit from her step-daughter's untimely death, as the money that would otherwise be held in trust and be inherited by the daughter will now pass to her."

" Hence her anxiety regarding a possible arrest for murder ? "

" Exactly so, at least in part. She, more than the mysteriously absent Mr. Colethorpe, would seem to enjoy a potent motive for the step-daughter's death. But before I begin to pronounce judgement on the matter, or indeed, before I take on the case fully, to the extent where I am prepared to pass judgement, we must await the results of the inquest. I informed her of this, and let her know that I will take no further action with regard to the case until official pronouncements on the manner and the cause of death had been made. By the by, I was mistaken. It is the violin and not the viola that she plays."

THE RESULTS OF THE AUTOPSY were published in the newspapers within the week, and I quote from a report published in the *Morning Post*, which I read to Sherlock Holmes as he reclined in his favourite armchair, his eyes half-closed as he listened.

" ' The jury of the inquest held on Miss Annabel Stevens, who died several days ago in her home in Reigate, has returned a verdict of murder by person or persons unknown. In his closing remarks to the jury, the coroner, Mr. Philip Draper, called attention to the analysis that had been performed of the contents of the dead woman's stomach. This had revealed a large quantity of an arsenical substance, commonly used in rat poisons. It was revealed by the step-mother of the deceased, who gave her name as Louise Montpensier, that her step-daughter had consumed little food at the meals served during the day, and this was confirmed by the stomach's being virtually empty, as discovered by Professor James Menzies, who performed the post-mortem examination of the body. However, she had not been described as being in poor spirits, either by Mme. Montpensier, or by the domestics who were summoned as witnesses concerning the deceased's mental state.' For what it is worth, I could see clearly for myself at the autopsy that the stomach contained less in the way of contents than might be expected."

" That may or may not be of significance," broke in Holmes. " Naturally, any poison would work faster on an empty stomach. Continue."

I resumed my reading. " ' In addition, the coroner had earlier drawn the jury's attention to a piece of paper, confirmed by an expert in the science of handwriting to have been written by the deceased, expressing the writer's discovery of a bitter taste in a beverage she had imbibed, and a fear of an unknown nocturnal visitor. When questioned as to the probable identity of the personage mentioned in the above note, Mme. Montpensier replied that she was positive it was her husband, Mr. Ferdinand Colethorpe, described as a man of business, who had been absent from the family home for some two months prior to the death of Miss Stevens. In answer to the coroner's questions, Mme. Montpensier professed herself unable to name the whereabouts of her husband. Mme. Montpensier also revealed under questioning that she had presented the dead girl with a drink of cocoa shortly before the latter retired on the night of her death.

" ' Given these circumstances, the foreman of the jury brought in the verdict of murder, and we believe the case has now been referred to Scotland Yard, where it is in the hands of Inspector Lestrade of the Metropolitan Police.' "

" And a pretty mess he will make of it, too, if I am not mistaken," remarked my friend. " Unless, that is, he has the sense to consult me on the matter."

" How do you intend to proceed ? " I asked, curiously.

" For the present, I shall do nothing. Nothing, that is, that has any relevance to this case. There is a monograph that I am writing that requires my attention for the morning, and a concert of late 18th-century Italian music this afternoon. If you would care to attend the latter with me, I would naturally be delighted. As to the former, I would be grateful if you would refrain from speech for the next few hours."

Such an utterance would have been offensive to me had it issued from any mouth other than that of Sherlock Holmes, but I was sufficiently familiar with my friend's crochets and fancies to regard this as commonplace. I myself was painfully aware that there were serious deficiencies in my medical knowledge, and I spent the morning immersed in the latest editions of the medical journals. Holmes in the meantime toiled away at his monograph, the subject of which he had previously informed me was connected with those peculiar characteristics of personality and habit that might be deduced from an inspection of the owner's umbrella or walking stick.

After we had partaken of the luncheon served to us by Mrs. Hudson, Holmes and I ventured forth to the concert hall, where we listened to one of the foremost fiddlers of the day perform his musical gymnastics upon his instrument. I fear that I, whose ear for music is untutored, and not always appreciative, fail to recall the name of the performer or that of any of the works which we heard on that occasion. I do recall vividly, though, Holmes' seemingly complete abstraction from the affairs of every day, and his languid pose as he drank in the abstruse sounds of the maestro.

As we exited the concert hall, Holmes humming to himself the theme of the last piece which we had heard, a familiar voice came from behind us.

" Mr. Holmes ! A word with you, if you please."

We turned, and beheld the earnest face of Inspector Lestrade, topped by his customary bowler, looking up at us.

" Ill met by moonlight, Inspector," Holmes answered him, amiably enough. " I take it this is not a chance meeting ? "

" By no means," replied Lestrade. " I wished to speak with you on a certain matter, and accordingly made my way to Baker-street. Your good landlady informed me that you were not at home, but was unable to inform me of your destination. She did, however, mention that you had left the house wearing your opera hat. On examining the list of concerts and entertainments on offer this afternoon, I rapidly came to the conclusion that this was the one where you were most likely to form a member of the audience, given the performer and the nature of the performance. I therefore waited outside the hall until the end of the concert, and—here we are."

" Well, well ! " said Holmes, chuckling. " I am not only impressed with your acumen, Lestrade, but also with your ability to learn and apply powers of deductive reasoning. I am surprised that you require my assistance."

Lestrade smiled in return. " I am glad that I could impress you somewhat. This latest case that has been brought to my attention demands a little more thought, however, and your assistance would be welcome."

" If it is the case in Reigate on which the coroner's jury has just pronounced a verdict, I fear I am unable to help you."

" How is that ? " answered Lestrade, visibly taken aback by the answer. " It is indeed that on which I wish to consult you."

" Pray, return with us to Baker-street," invited Holmes. " We can discuss this at more length in comfort."

Lestrade accepted the invitation, and we returned to our lodgings, where a warm fire was blazing.

" Now, Lestrade, tell me what you have discovered so far," invited Holmes, when we were comfortably settled in our chairs. " I must warn you, though, that I have been engaged by Mme. Montpensier to clear her of the charge of murder that she fears will be brought against her."

Lestrade furrowed his brow. " There is no charge pending against her. I have never heard of such a thing, though I confess that circumstances point to her involvement in the death. It smacks to me, Mr. Holmes, of a guilty conscience."

" I am somewhat puzzled by the affair myself, believe me. What problems particularly concern you in this matter ? "

" Well, to start, the whole business of the missing husband has got me puzzled, I confess," began Lestrade. " He is obviously the prime suspect in this case, and we have been unable to discover hide or hair of the man. He appears to have vanished from the face of the earth."

Holmes laughed. " Tush ! You are puzzled by this ? There is a second Mrs. Colethorpe, if the man has been foolish enough to use the same name for both his marriages. He is living the classic life of a bigamist. Mme. Montpensier is not the primary object of his affections, though, if her account to me is to be believed. It is clear that he spends the majority of his time elsewhere, doubtless with his other household. However, the money that Montpensier's first husband left to his daughter, and to the family generally, almost certainly play a part in his decision to tie the nuptial knot for a second time."

Lestrade's face fell a little at this announcement. " So you believe that we will never find him ? "

" He will do his best to stay away from Mme. Montpensier and the general area of Reigate for some time. I am sure he will not wish to draw undue attention to himself."

" So you believe him to be guilty of the crime ? "

" To what crime are you referring ? "

" Why, that of murder, as determined by the coroner's jury."

" I would remind you, Inspector," remarked Holmes calmly, " that although the jury returned a verdict of murder by person or persons unknown, and therefore you are bound to search for the murderer, there is as yet no definite proof that a murder was committed."

Lestrade let out a snort of amusement. " A poisoned girl, with a letter indicating her terror and fear, detailing how she partook of a drink that was poisoned, and you tell me it's not murder ? "

" I did not say that. I said there was no proof as yet that a murder has been committed. Accidental death or suicide are alternative explanations. Coroners' juries are hardly infallible. I should let you know, though, that if the cause of death does appear to be murder, and if my client's guilt seems proven, then she will cease to be my client, and I will cease to act on her behalf. I am sure you understand me well enough, Inspector, to know that I have no interest in hindering the course of justice."

" I am confident that you will provide us with every assistance, as you have in the past," answered the little man. " To start, would you recommend that we continue our search for the missing husband ? "

" I would think it advisable. He has, after all, almost as strong a motive as my client for making away with his step-daughter. I take it you are familiar with the clauses of the will of Mme. Montpensier's first husband ? " Lestrade shook his head, and Holmes proceeded to enlighten him with the facts as they had been related to us.

" Well, well. That does seem to provide both the husband and wife with a powerful motive," said Lestrade thoughtfully. " Are there any other beneficiaries who would profit ? "

" As far as I am aware, there are none. Tell me, Inspector, have you visited the scene of the death ? "

" As yet, no. It was chiefly about this that I wished your assistance. I am aware that you have had some luck in the past when discovering clues on similar occasions and making guesses that have been of assistance to us." I noted Holmes' visible irritation at this description of his work, but Lestrade continued, seemingly oblivious of the offence he had caused. " The inquest seems to have been conducted remarkably badly. There are many questions which I would have raised had I been present, and which remain unanswered. I would be obliged if you would be present at Reigate and meet me there tomorrow morning."

" I was intending to make that visit in any case," Holmes replied stiffly. " Tomorrow morning at nine ? "

" Admirable," Lestrade said. " You may care to look through this," presenting a sheaf of papers to Holmes. " It is a transcript of the evidence that was presented at the inquest. As I say, there are many omissions, which I hope to remedy tomorrow."

Holmes thanked Lestrade, who took his hat and left us.

" The man becomes more intolerable by the week ! " exclaimed Holmes angrily. " ' Luck' and ' guesses', indeed ! Anyone other than a blockhead who has worked with me as often as has Lestrade should be able to recognise that my methods are based on scientific deduction. Were it not for the fact that Mme. Montpensier is my client, I would have refused outright to accompany him." So saying, he picked up his pipe, and lit it with a spill composed of some unanswered correspondence, which he lit from the fire. " Pah ! " he resumed his tirade, all the while filling the room with the blue smoke from his pipe. " I cannot begin to comprehend the depths of ignorance and stupidity to which our police sink at times. To treat the science of detection as a mere plaything—a bagatelle—is an attitude which is simply beyond my understanding."

I could think of no satisfactory rejoinder to this, and allowed him to continue his expostulations against the perceived foolishness of the Metropolitan Police in general, and Inspector Lestrade as a particular exemplar. These opinions were not unfamiliar to me, and I admit that they had lost their interest along with their novelty. It was with a start, therefore, that I realised that Holmes was addressing me directly.

" I am sorry, I failed to catch your words."

" So I remarked," he said tartly. " I was asking you whether, in your opinion as a medical man, the symptoms you observed in the corpse were those which are consistent with arsenic poisoning."

" I would have to say so, though certain aspects were not wholly typical. If the source of the poison was indeed commercial rat poison, then one might well expect other substances to be present, and the combination of the arsenic, the presence of which was no doubt confirmed in the laboratory through the use of a Marsh's apparatus, with the other ingredients used in the preparation would no doubt produce effects of an unknown nature."

" We will discover more tomorrow, no doubt," replied Holmes, and returned to his reflections while leafing through the papers that had been supplied to him by Lestrade.

※※※※

HE NEXT DAY saw us travelling to Reigate, where we made our rendezvous with Lestrade as had been previously arranged. Mme. Montpensier welcomed us, and made the dining-room available to us. Her appearance remained as of one who had suffered a severe shock to the system, and her face bore evidence of the grief at her loss. It was impossible for me to regard her as the murderer of her own step-daughter, however strong the evidence against her might appear to be.

" Where shall we start ? " asked Lestrade of Holmes. The little inspector seemed more unsure of his own abilities than he had the previous evening.

" Since you have yet to interview Madame Montpensier yourself, I would suggest that this would seem a logical place to begin your enquiries here. I would make the request, though I realise that you are within your rights to refuse, that Dr. Watson and I remain in the room during your questioning."

" Very well," answered Lestrade, and requested me to bring Mme. Montpensier to the room. On entering, Lestrade, with more gentleness than was usual for him, invited her to sit, and he commenced his questioning regarding the events of the morning on which the body had been discovered.

She answered him briefly and concisely, but at times interrupted by sobs, giving the same facts as she had previously reported to Holmes and myself when she had visited us at Baker-Street, and which she had repeated at the inquest. Lestrade then turned the subject to the terms of the will of her late husband, and the conditions under which the money would pass to her before raising the subject of the paper that had been found in the dead girl's room. Again, she insisted that the person mentioned in the note that had been discovered was her absent husband, Colethorpe. Throughout this testimony, her answers were entirely consistent with what we had heard earlier from her and the evidence she had given at the coroner's hearing. When she tearfully repeated that she could provide no more information, Lestrade dismissed her, and turned to Holmes.

" Weeping women are the very devil when it comes to obtaining useful information, are they not, Mr. Holmes ? I find it impossible to pursue any consistent line of enquiry with them."

" As is often their intention," remarked Holmes, sardonically.

" You believe she is withholding information from us ? "

" Without a doubt. As yet, I have no idea what that information may be, but since you have yet to interview the servants involved in this affair, I would suggest that we take our enquiries further by asking them about their impressions of the fateful morning. It has now been so long since the event that we can place little reliance on their memories for the exact facts, I fear, but we should at the least be able to obtain some general idea of the events of that night."

One Hannah Turvey, the maid who had entered the room first following Mme. Montpensier's discovery of the body, and who had then raised the alarm, was the first to be called. She was a woman of late middle-age, and had an air of solidity and dependability about her.

She could add little to what we had already been told, except when Holmes questioned her about the note that had been discovered.

" You found it on her dressing table, I believe ? "

" No, sir, I did not. It was lying on a small desk that stands by the window in her room."

" Did you say this to your mistress ? "

"I am not certain that I did so, sir. I may have simply said to Madame Montpensier that I discovered it in the room."

"No matter, it may prove to be of little significance. Let us turn now to the drink that was mentioned in the note. What drink would this be?"

"That would be Miss Annabel's hot cocoa, sir, which she always drank of an evening before she went to sleep."

"And you would prepare it for her?"

"Oh no, sir. That was Sarah's job—that is, the kitchen-maid, Sarah Nolan. That's what I said at the inquest."

"So you did. I simply wished to make certain of my facts. Why was that not the task of the cook?"

"Cook was almost always gone to bed by the time Miss Annabel was ready for her drink. Sarah would make the cocoa and hand it on a tray to Miss Annabel as she went to bed."

"This is all in the transcript of the inquest. In this case, it was not this Sarah who actually handed the cocoa to Miss Stevens, though," Lestrade pointed out to Holmes.

"I realise that, but it is always good to have these matters confirmed beyond reasonable doubt." He turned to the maid. "What happened to the cup in which the cocoa was served?" he demanded of her.

The servant appeared to start weeping. "You're not the first one to ask me that, sir," she answered him through her tears. "I had taken the tray downstairs that morning and given it to Sarah for washing before I knew what I had done."

"You had not read the note?"

"Yes, sir, I had. But it just came natural to me to

clean up. I had no thought of anything else." Her sobs broke out afresh.

" There, there," said Holmes kindly. " No-one can blame you under such circumstances."

" Thank you, sir," she sniffed.

" Tell me, Hannah, how long have you been in service here ? "

" I started with Madame Montpensier when she first came to this country. I was her maid and her dresser when she worked as a dancer, and when she married Mr. Stevens, I stayed as her maid and have continued in her service since then."

" She is a good mistress to you ? "

" The best a body could wish, sir. She has never been anything but kindness and generosity itself to me."

" That is good to hear, Hannah. Thank you. We may require further questions of you, but for now you are dismissed. Please send the kitchen-maid, Sarah, to us."

While we were waiting for Sarah Nolan to appear, Holmes turned to Lestrade. " It was culpable of her to dispose of what might have proved important evidence, but there is nothing to be gained by our taking the matter further. What's done is done, and cannot be put right now. We must now discover the exact circumstances under which the cocoa which was given to Miss Stevens was prepared by this Sarah."

As he finished speaking, the young woman in question—indeed, she was little more than a girl—entered. Her manner seemed subdued and hesitant, in contrast to her general appearance, which was one of youth and energy. Her face, when she raised it to look Lestrade in the eye, was attractive and might almost have been termed 'pretty', were it not for the dirt and grime consequent on her duties as a kitchen-maid.

"Now, Sarah," began Lestrade. "You usually prepared the cocoa for Miss Stevens and served it to her before she retired for the night. Is that correct ? "

The girl looked down at the floor. "Yes, sir," she mumbled.

"And you did so on the night that Miss Stevens died ? "

"No, sir, I did not. I did not prepare it, and the mistress has said herself, hasn't she, that she gave it to Miss Annabel." Her voice was a little clearer, and she raised her head to look Sherlock Holmes in the eye.

Lestrade sat forward in his seat. "Why did you not mention this at the inquest ? "

"Nobody asked me, sir."

The little policeman sighed heavily and slumped back in his chair. "Mr. Holmes, please continue."

My friend took up the questioning again. "So, Sarah," he said gently to the girl, who now appeared somewhat terrified. "If you did not give the cocoa to Miss Stevens, who did so ? "

"It was the mistress, sir. Mrs. Colethorpe. I'd started to make the cocoa as I usually do, and had just put the cup on the tray before putting in the hot milk to mix in with the cocoa powder. I was just about to start when Mrs. Colethorpe walked into the kitchen."

"Did she often come into the kitchen ? "

"Quite often, sir. She usually came in to talk to Cook, and to give orders for that day's meals and that sort of thing. It wasn't common for her to come in at that time of night, but it wasn't the first time, either, by a long way. Sometimes she liked to make the cocoa, and of course, I couldn't say ' no' to her when she got that sort of fancy in her head."

" What time was this ? "

" It was about half-past ten, sir. In fact, I remember the clock in the hall striking as the milk came to the boil. Made me jump a bit, it did, and I almost spilled some of the milk."

" I see," said Holmes. " And what did she say to you when she came in ? "

" I can't remember exactly, sir, but it was something like, ' Don't worry about that, Sarah, I'll make sure she gets it.' And then she started to make the cocoa. Then she picked up the tray and walked out of the kitchen with it."

" Was this the first time she had done this ? "

" Oh, Lord love you, sir, not at all. I won't say it was common for her to do this, because it wasn't, but it wasn't the first time, like I said to you just now."

" Did you see her give the tray to Miss Stevens ? "

The kitchen-maid shook her head. " No, sir. She took the tray and walked out of the kitchen with it. I stayed in the kitchen and cleaned up after making the cocoa. If I leave the things till the next morning, Cook gets terrible angry with me."

Holmes smiled at her. " I am sure she does, and I am sure that she will be angry with me if I keep you from your duties for much longer. Two more questions. How do you usually prepare the cocoa, and on that night, was the way you were going to prepare the cocoa in any way different from the usual ? "

The girl appeared to regard the question with a little wonder. " Why, sir, I was going to make it just the same as I usually do. That is, I boiled up the milk and then I was going to mix a little with the cocoa powder, and add a spoonful of sugar. Then I usually add the rest of the hot milk, and mix it all up. That's the way I've always done it, and I can tell you that I wasn't going to make any changes on that night."

" You watched your mistress prepare the drink ? Did she make it in that way ? "

" I was cleaning up some things, sir, but I did notice her making the cocoa while I was doing that. Mixing the cocoa powder with a bit of the milk, and then adding the milk, and a few spoons of sugar, like she usually did. There was nothing strange about it, except that the sugar went in after, which is different to the way I do it, like I say. Nothing that I would not have done myself, really."

" Thank you. That is most helpful. We may ask you more questions in the future, but for the moment, you are free to go, unless the Inspector here has any further questions."

" If I may, sir— ? " It was clear that there was something more of which she wished to inform us.

" Well ? "

" The next morning, I was preparing for the breakfast. Cook does the cooking, but it is my job to make the kitchen ready, and to fetch the milk and so on. I was in the pantry, and I noticed Mrs. Colethorpe coming into the kitchen."

" What time was this ? " Lestrade asked her.

" I hadn't been up and about for more than about thirty minutes. I am not certain of the exact time, but it would be about half-past six."

" Did you speak to her ? "

" No, sir, I did not. She was coming in all secret-like,

as though she didn't want to be seen. She was carrying the jar in which we keep the sugar in the kitchen."

" You are positive about that ? "

" Why, yes, sir. It's a blue and white pottery jar, and it has the word ' Sugar' written on it. There was no mistaking it."

" Why would it be out of the kitchen ? Did you see her remove it on the previous night when she made the cocoa ? "

" No, sir. I put that jar back on the shelf myself, after she'd carried the tray with the cocoa to Miss Annabel."

" And was it missing when you entered the kitchen the next morning ? "

" I didn't notice, sir."

" And it is there now ? "

" Yes, sir, it is. But the strange thing is that I saw Mrs. Colethorpe leave the kitchen that morning, and she was carrying the same jar with her when she went out of the kitchen. When she had gone, I went straight to the place where the sugar jar is kept, and it was still there."

" And there is only the one jar of that type ? " Lestrade demanded.

" Yes, sir. I have never seen any other jar in this household of that shape and colour with the word ' Sugar' on it."

" I see," said Holmes. " I think I have no more questions for now. Inspector ? "

Lestrade shook his head, and the girl left us.

" Why, in the name of everything, could this not all have come out at the inquest ? " said Lestrade. " All that was asked was ' Did you usually make the cocoa for Miss Stevens ? '"

" To which she naturally answered, ' Yes,'" said Holmes. " In her defence, it may be said that she did, after all, tell the truth, the whole truth, and nothing but the truth."

" And why in the name of thunder did Montpensier not tell us that she had made the cocoa herself ? "

" I would have thought that was somewhat obvious, Inspector. She had no wish to incriminate herself still further. I agree that the case against her is looking rather black. This business of the sugar jar—or rather the jars, for there can be no doubt that there is more than one such in the case—is a totally unexpected twist."

" I think we may conclude that one of those jars contained poison together with the sugar, and was then replaced with one containing sugar alone by Mme. Montpensier early in the morning when she believed herself to be unobserved," said Lestrade.

" That would indeed seem to be a logical deduction. I would remind you though, Inspector, that there has been ample opportunity for the disposal of the jar containing the poison. I am certain there is nothing now present in the kitchen that will confirm this report. Furthermore, we have only the word of this one servant girl to inform us of this action."

" Do you suspect her of lying ? Of fabricating this story ? "

" I suspect her motives in concealing this information until now. Why did she not volunteer this information earlier ? She seems to have her wits about her."

" Because she was never asked these exact questions, as you said ? " I suggested.

" Quite possibly that is the sole reason, though I find it hard to credit. She seems to be a girl of some intelligence, and to understand the possible consequences of what she was saying to us."

" In any case," Lestrade broke in, " we should pay a visit downstairs to the kitchen and see this mysterious jar for ourselves."

The basement kitchen was occupied by the cook, Mrs. Gresham, who obviously resented the intrusion into her domain by three middle-aged gentlemen.

" If you're the police, I want you to understand that I was in bed that night. I had a cold, and the mistress told me I should take myself to bed early. As soon as I had served up the dinner for the mistress and Miss Annabel, I took myself to bed. That was about eight o'clock."

" My dear Mrs. Gresham," said Holmes. " No-one is accusing you of anything. We merely wished to see how you keep your kitchen and your pantry."

" Well, I'm sure you're welcome," she sniffed. " If you are going to go poking around, you've got to put back everything exactly where you found it, mind."

" Rest assured that your kitchen will be left in the state we discovered it," Holmes told her. " But maybe you can help us, and prevent us from disturbing you excessively by showing us where the cocoa and all the other ingredients for that drink are located."

" The cocoa is kept in this tin here, as you can see," she said, leading us to a shelf, where the distinctively printed tin stood. The milk would come from the can here, and for them as likes sugar, it's here."

We examined the container, which was exactly as had been described to us earlier, and Holmes, with the permission of the cook, took a sample of its contents which he placed in an envelope, Lestrade doing the same.

"I fear that this will not produce any results, though," he muttered as he sealed the envelope. " I think we may be certain that this contains sugar alone." He addressed himself to the cook. " Sarah would boil the milk for the cocoa at the range here ? "

" She would."

" Thank you. Would you mind telling us what you gave your mistress and Miss Stevens for dinner that night ? "

Her eyes narrowed. " I hope you're not suggesting that it was my cooking that killed Miss Annabel ? "

" By no means. How could it be when your mistress is alive and well ? They both partook of the same food, I am sure."

" Well, sir, yes they did. It was a light meal. Neither of them is a big eater at that hour, so I gave them some clear broth to start with, and they both had some of that, so Hannah told me."

" Excuse me," interrupted Lestrade. " May we take it that Hannah, Miss Stevens' maid, served the meal to them ? "

" That's right, sir. She did that. So, as I was saying, they started with the soup and then I gave them a nice bit of haddock, poached in milk, with potatoes and carrots and sprouts. And I used the milk I'd used for the fish to make a nice parsley sauce to go with it. I always say you can't beat a nice parsley sauce to go with haddock cooked that way."

" Indeed so," agreed Holmes, smiling.

" There was a savoury of devils on horseback, and then they had stewed plums."

" And both partook of all the dishes ? "

" That they did, but Miss Annabel was never a heavy eater, and she didn't eat much that night."

" Did they take any wine or anything to drink with the meal ? "

" The mistress, being French, liked a drop of wine with her food. No more than a glass with a meal. Miss Annabel, though, she never touched a drop. She would have water. And the mistress had water as well as her wine," she added. " Don't go thinking it was the water that did it."

" Naturally, I would think no such thing," protested Holmes. " I think that answers my questions. Inspector ? "

" I have nothing further to ask at present," replied Lestrade.

We made our way upstairs to the ground floor, where we were met by Mme. Montpensier.

" Have you discovered evidence of his guilt ? " she asked us, stammering in obvious fear.

" I am unable to comment on the progress of our investigations," Lestrade told her, stiffly.

" Mr. Holmes," our client implored my friend. " Cannot you tell me more ? "

" Believe me, Madame," said Holmes gently, " when I say that if I could tell you more, I would certainly do so, but I do not feel that I am in a position to give you any firm pronouncements."

" I understand," she said simply, and walked away from us without a further word.

" Do you remember, Mr. Holmes," enquired Lestrade, as she disappeared round a corner of the passage, " the report on the poison swallowed by the deceased ? "

"Naturally. It was assumed to be some form of rat poison, was it not?"

"Indeed it was, Mr. Holmes. And I noticed mouse-traps in the kitchen. Where there are mice, there are also rats, are there not?"

"Often that turns out to be the case," Holmes conceded.

"It is my belief that we will find rat poison if we search this house, and when we submit it to analysis, we will discover it to be identical to the contents of the deceased's stomach."

"That, Lestrade, may well indicate how she died. It does not tell us who was the agent of her death."

"Oh, Mr. Holmes! It is obvious, is it not? It is the step-mother. Consider. She has the motive—the will that leaves a substantial sum to her in the event of her step-daughter's death. She has the means—the rat poison which I am confident I will find. And she had the opportunity—it was she prepared the fatal drink and who carried the tray with it to her step-daughter. I tell you, Mr. Holmes, once I have discovered that poison, all the links in the chain are complete, and she will then stand trial for her crimes."

"You are leaping to premature conclusions, Inspector. I warn you that your case will hardly stand up in court. Much more work needs to be done before you can make an arrest. By the by, I have not yet seen the original of that note that was found. Do you have it on your person?"

Lestrade reached inside his coat, and produced a large brown envelope containing a folded piece of paper, which he passed to Holmes, who withdrew the paper and commenced studying the writing, which covered both sides of it, with the aid of his powerful lens.

" This has been folded since it was given to you. I am surprised at you, Lestrade, to tamper with possible evidence in this way," said Holmes, obviously annoyed.

" How in the world would you know that ? "

" So much is obvious from even a cursory inspection of the fibres of the paper and the way they are arranged, and the manner in which have picked up fibres from the envelope in which the paper has been stored. But no matter. The handwriting is definitely that of the deceased ? "

" There can be no doubt there. An independent expert has testified that this writing is that of Miss Stevens, after having compared it with other samples."

" We may take it, then, that she wrote these words. Using a steel-nibbed pen, as you have no doubt noted, and a slightly unusual shade of blue-black ink. You have confirmed that she was left-handed ? " Lestrade shook his head. " My dear Inspector, how can we hope to solve these puzzles if you will not take the trouble to confirm even the most elementary facts ? "

" It had not occurred to me that she was left-handed," confessed the hapless police inspector.

" No matter. And the paper ? "

" A simple sheet of notepaper, no more."

Holmes smote his forehead. " God has given you eyes, man ! Observe and take note. This is not a standard size of paper, as I am sure even you have noted. One side has been cut, with a pair of short-bladed scissors with curved blades. Nail-scissors, I am certain. There are still, despite your mangling of the sheet, traces of the curve of the paper when it was bound into a notebook."

" This is a page cut from a notebook, then ? " I asked.

" That is what I am saying. So much is evident to even the meanest intelligence." It was obvious to both Lestrade and myself that Holmes' patience was wearing thin, and to create a diversion in his thoughts, I proposed that we move upstairs to the chamber which had been occupied by Miss Stevens, and in which her body had been discovered.

As Lestrade and I trailed up the stairs behind Sherlock Holmes, Lestrade turned to me and whispered in my ear. " Thank you for that diversion, Doctor. Mr. Holmes does not appear to be in the best of tempers today."

" I am afraid that you put yourself on his wrong side yesterday when you mentioned ' luck' and ' guesswork'. As you know, he regards detection as a matter of scientific enquiry rather than as a matter of luck."

" I understand," said Lestrade. " I will endeavour to be a little more circumspect in my speech in the future."

By this time, Holmes had entered the room, and was standing at the desk which had been mentioned by the servant as the place where the note had been discovered. " This is most curious," he remarked, standing in front of the secretaire, which was well provided with paper, envelopes, fountain pens, and ink. " Tell me, Watson, why would one choose to eat soup with a fork ? Or to plant a large tree using a small trowel with which to dig the hole ? "

These questions came as riddles to me. " I have no idea." I was perplexed. " Indeed, I have not the faintest conception of to what it is that you are referring." Lestrade glanced at me, and when Holmes, once again turning his back to us, bent to re-examine the desk and its contents, he moved his forefinger in a circular motion beside his temple. While not sharing Lestrade's opinion of Holmes' mental instability, I was nonetheless more than a little perplexed by Holmes' actions.

Suddenly, Holmes turned to face us, and addressed himself to Lestrade. " You may ignore that piece of paper, Inspector," Holmes told the policeman. " To a certain extent, that is."

" I have no notion of what it is that you mean by your words. The note was found on that desk, was it not ? "

" So we are led to believe."

" And was written by Miss Stevens while seated at that desk ? "

" Very possibly."

" Then I fail to comprehend what you are saying to me."

Holmes did not reply, but merely shrugged. " I have seen what I expected to see and drawn my conclusions. You, my dear Lestrade, have seen exactly what I have seen, but have failed to draw your own conclusions, other than the obvious ones, which are sadly in error in this instance."

" You believe Mme. Montpensier did not kill her step-daughter ? "

" I believe her to be innocent of murder," replied Holmes simply. " I would advise you now, for the sake of your career and your reputation, to refrain from making any arrests at this time. Can I persuade you to stay your hand for at least two days ? "

" Since it is you, Mr. Holmes, I will trust your judgement here. I feel, though, that I should conduct a search for the missing container which we believe contained the poison."

"That would seem to me to be an excellent plan, Lestrade. It is one which I do not propose to carry out myself, having full confidence that you and your men will perform it competently and thoroughly."

"What do you propose to do, then?"

"I will examine the effects of Mme. Montpensier's present husband that he keeps in this house for his use when he deigns to make an appearance."

"Each to his own, but you seem to believe that the note discovered in the dead woman's room is of no importance," objected Lestrade.

"Think carefully on my exact words," were Holmes' words as he turned on his heel. "Come, Watson. Let us seek permission for our errand from Madame."

This permission was readily granted. "For all I care, you may take his effects and make a bonfire of them in the garden at the back of the house," she told us.

"What exactly do you hope to gain from this?" I asked Holmes as we entered the dressing-room.

"Even the most competent of criminals makes mistakes sometimes. We know this man as Ferdinand Colethorpe, do we not? I have a strong suspicion that if we make a search of his belongings here, we will find some sort of evidence that will lead us to his other identity."

"And you believe him to be involved here? After what we have heard about Mme. Montpensier's actions?"

"It is precisely because of those actions that I say this."

I was much puzzled by these words, but assisted him in his search of the missing man's belongings for any clue that might lead us to an identity other than that of Ferdinand Colethorpe. It was I who discovered a pair of cuff-links with the initials "T.R.". "These would appear to be the kind of item for which you are searching," I said, holding them out to Holmes.

" Indeed so," said Holmes. " In point of fact, being such personal items, I feel sure that these initials will be the ones which he is using elsewhere." It was Holmes himself who presently discovered a small pile of correspondence, the bulk of which was addressed to Mr. Ferdinand Colethorpe, but in the centre of which was a letter from a firm of builders addressed to a Mr. Thomas Richards, at an address in Holborn, dated not some two months previously.

" I will wager that Mr. Richards is our man," said Holmes.

" I fail to see your reasoning, even so," replied I. " We have no reason to believe he was anywhere near this place on the night of his step-daughter's death."

" Indeed so. This would be the last place I would expect him to have been at that time. Indeed, when we meet him, I expect him to present us with a complete alibi, which may be verified by reference to a number of completely reliable and trustworthy witnesses."

" And yet you say he is involved in this mystery ? "

" He is the key."

" So you do not believe that Mme. Montpensier is the murderess ? "

" I said before, and I repeat now, that if my clients are demonstrably proven to be guilty, they do not remain my clients. Mme. Montpensier remains my client."

" And yet we have so much evidence to point to her involvement. The poison must have been administered in the cocoa, must it not ? "

" I agree that it is the most likely vehicle, yes."

" And she prepared it and delivered it to her daughter."

" That is so."

" I fail to understand."

" All will be revealed, never fear. Aha ! Here is Lestrade, and I believe he, too, has found success to crown his efforts."

The police inspector came bustling up to us. " Under the rhododendrons, Mr. Holmes." He held out for our inspection, a fragment of blue and white earthenware, with an air of triumph. " And the dry weather we have been enjoying lately has ensured that there is enough of the contents remaining for a sample to be taken for analysis."

" Excellent. And I have a name and an address for you." He passed over the correspondence that he had discovered.

" Oho ! " cried Lestrade. " We should question him about his movements on the night of the death."

" That, as I remarked to Watson just now, would be a waste of time. I am convinced that he was demonstrably some way from here when the death occurred. You will get nothing useful from him in that direction. However, feel free to question Mr. Richards. I would like to be present at that event, if I may."

" That can be arranged," said Lestrade. " I will send a telegram to the Yard immediately, asking for Mr. Richards to be escorted to a suitable place."

" And now," said Holmes, as the excited Lestrade left us, " it is time for us to talk with our client. If I am to save her from the gallows, I need some answers which will help me establish her innocence."

We entered the drawing-room, in which we discovered Mme. Montpensier, engaged in reading a book. Invited to sit, Holmes remained standing, his back to the fire, as he engaged her in conversation.

" Madame," he began. " You must understand that if I am to help you, I require the truth from you. I wish to have your confirmation, for example, that you are well aware that it was you who killed your step-daughter and destroyed the evidence that you had done so."

I sprang from my chair. " This is infamous, Holmes ! " I exclaimed. " You cannot make such accusations without proof ! "

" I have sufficient proof," replied Sherlock Holmes coldly, regarding Mme. Montpensier, who was now weeping bitterly.

" Yes, Mr. Holmes, I killed her. But you should know that it was never my intention to do so, and I have no way of proving who did it. But it was not I who meant to bring about her death, even though I was the instrument of it."

" This is where I can help you," said Holmes, in his calmest and most gentle tones. " Madame," he continued, taking her by the elbows, and staring into her tearful eyes, " you have been the victim of as despicable a felony as I have ever encountered. My greatest wish is to see those responsible brought to justice."

" Then you know all ? " asked the wretched woman, some hope creeping into her voice.

" No, but I will tell you what I know, and you will tell me if I am correct or not. On the night that your daughter died, she was feeling unwell. We have the cook's words, as relayed by your maid Hannah, that she partook of a light supper."

" That is so."

" Out of concern for her health, or for whatever reason

prompted by your maternal feelings for the girl, you determined to prepare her night-time drink of cocoa, a task which you had performed in the past, and was unusual, but not unprecedented. The maid Sarah was in the kitchen, having made the preliminary preparations for the drink." Our client nodded. " You made the drink in the usual way, adding hot milk and sugar to the cocoa powder and handing the drink to your step-daughter. At what point did you realise that the drink had been poisoned, and that it was the sugar that was to blame ? "

" It was when I myself retired some hours later. All the servants had retired for the night. In my wardrobe I discovered the very sugar container that I had left in the kitchen earlier that evening, or so it seemed to me. In a flash, it occurred to me that something was amiss. The only reason I could consider was that the sugar in the kitchen was not what it purported to be, and the jar had been substituted with some sinister purpose in mind."

" How probably was it that the jar of sugar was to be discovered in your room by you ? "

" Not very likely, I would say. It was only because I was searching for a bed-jacket that I wished to wear that I happened upon it."

" You may depend on it that it would have been found if the police had searched your room," said Holmes, " thereby adding more supposed evidence to convict you. A truly diabolical mind is behind this. Pray continue."

" I never take sugar in coffee or tea or any other drink. Indeed, my body seems to revolt against any sugar."

" I take it you are a sufferer from diabetes ? " I enquired.

She nodded in agreement. " So I have been told by

Dr. Clifford. In any case, my dislike of sugar in food is well-known to the household, and the sugar is reserved for the use of Annabel alone. Any form of foul play in which the sugar played a part would be directed against her. All this came to me in a flash. Colethorpe, my absent husband, had in the past mentioned the dangers of storing rat poison in the kitchen. It was almost as if he were warning me of his intentions, which I knew to be evil. Do not tell me how I knew this, Mr. Holmes. You may call it women's intuition, but I knew." She sobbed violently, and seemed incapable of speech for a while.

" Compose yourself," Holmes urged her. " Pray tell us what happened next, and we will ensure that those responsible are brought to justice."

I had no wish at that time of night to go down once more to the kitchen in the dark, and discover for myself what had happened." Holmes lifted his eyebrows a little. " To tell you the truth, Mr. Holmes, it was not that I had no wish to make the journey downstairs, but I was terrified. I had by this time convinced myself that something was amiss, and I made my way to the door outside Annabel's room. I knew that something was amiss," she repeated, " but I was a coward, Mr. Holmes. I could not bear the thought of my beloved Annabel suffering, but at the same time I knew in my bones that I was not capable of preventing what had probably already occurred. I could not enter that room. And there was another consideration. It came to me that I was the one who would be blamed for her death and if I were to be seen entering or leaving her room... I lay awake all night, unable to sleep, and fearful of the morrow. As the day broke, I knew that I had to return the sugar to the pantry. I slipped down, unseen by anyone—"

" The kitchen-maid Sarah claims to have seen you."

" She is a liar ! " spat out our client. " The lazy little hussy was still in her bed, I am certain of it."

" She has just given a most detailed account to the police," said Holmes. " Even if she were lying, I am sure that she would have no hesitation about repeating her story under oath."

" Why would she do such a thing ? " enquired Mme. Montpensier in bewilderment.

" That is an answer I hope to be able to discover in the very near future, Madame. It may be an answer that may be painful to your ears, however."

" What could be more painful than the agonies I have suffered so far ? " demanded the miserable woman. " Nothing ! I beg of you, Mr. Holmes, to spare me nothing when you discover the truth."

Holmes inclined his head. " It is my opinion, Madame, that you have been mightily wronged, and I will therefore tell you all as it comes to light. Please continue your narrative, which so far corresponds precisely to my deductions."

" I discovered a duplicate container in the accustomed place in the kitchen. I opened it, and the sugar in there appeared, other than one small part, to be as it should be. There was a subtle difference in texture, which could not have been detected by the lamplight the previous evening when I prepared the cocoa, but was apparent in the morning daylight. If I had not been wearing my pince-nez—the ones I left behind me when I visited you in London—I would never have seen anything. I was not wearing them the previous night when I prepared Annabel's drink."

" Aha ! " cried Holmes. " Observe the cunning with

which this trap was set. It would have been a relatively simple matter to mix sufficient poison throughout the whole of the sugar, but they merely sprinkled a concentration on top of the container, meaning that it would be almost impossible to detect the presence of the poison in the container once the fatal dose had been administered. It would then appear, Madame, as if you had deliberately added a spoonful of the rat poison, for this is what appears to have been the fatal agent, to the cocoa. Had the whole of the sugar been laced, or replaced, with the poison, there would also have been an obvious danger of ingestion by those for whom the poison was not intended, and the death of your step-daughter might have been considered the result of a tragic accident. The method adopted makes the action look more deliberate." He paused, allowing Mme. Montpensier and myself to consider his words before he continued. " What did you do with the substitute container containing the adulterated sugar ? "

" I hurried outside and smashed it to smithereens, hiding the pieces under the rhododendrons. The sugar spilled over the ground, and I was unable to hide it. I knew it was inevitable that I would be revealed as the one who had prepared the fatal beverage and given it to my Annabel. Why it was not revealed at the inquest, I have no idea, but now believe that it was part of this plot to incriminate me. However, can you blame me for wanting to hide my actions ? "

" Madame, it is a serious matter to conceal the truth from the law, even when the truth may not be incriminating. The fact that you have covered up your part in this tragedy until now has probably convinced the police of your guilt as a murderess. I am currently attempting to establish your innocence in their eyes, and I must remind you once more that I require your full cooperation to accomplish this."

" I understand," she replied meekly.

" The police have discovered both the shards of the sugar jar, and the remains of the sugar that it contained. From what you tell us, though, the sugar may well be harmless, and the poison will not appear in any laboratory tests that may be carried out on it. Pray continue with your narrative."

" After I had disposed of the fatal jar, I went back inside. It was cold in the garden, and I was shaking, but not with cold. It was with terror, Mr. Holmes. Terror of what I might discover, and terror of being falsely accused, and being unable to defend myself against such false accusations. I steeled myself to learn the worst, and made my way to Annabel's room, to discover her a lifeless corpse, and to realise that I—I who loved her as if I were her own mother—had been the instrument of her death ! " At this, her sobs broke out anew, and it was pitiful to behold this woman, who appeared to be the victim of as foul a plot as can be imagined. " From there," she eventually continued, " I have told you the rest. Overcome with shame at my own cowardice, and horror at what had occurred, I fainted, and was revived by my maid, Hannah."

" Let us discuss the question of your servants, if we may," said Holmes. " Hannah told us that she had been your dresser at the time of your theatrical career, and has remained in your service since then."

" That is correct. Hannah is a dear soul to me, and has helped me through many a bad time. She was as devoted to Annabel as I was, and it is my opinion that she grieves for the girl as much as I do myself."

" Very well. I take it that Sarah was originally in Mr. Colethorpe's service, and joined your household when you married him ? The cook, Mrs. Gresham, I take to have been employed when you married Mr. Stevens."

" That is correct on both counts."

" How in the world could you know that, Holmes ? " I could not refrain from asking.

" By the way in which they referred to Mme. Montpensier here. Hannah referred to her as ' Mme. Montpensier' with an air of being familiar with the true French pronunciation. It was obviously an appellation with which she was familiar. Since you informed us that you had only recently reverted to that name, I knew that she had a long acquaintance with you, even before she confirmed this with her own lips. On the other hand, Mrs. Gresham used only the terms ' my mistress' or ' the mistress' in her conversation with us. All very well and proper, one might think, for a new servant, or one in Mrs. Gresham's position, but it was obvious to me, though, when we visited the kitchen, that all had been arranged for the benefit of the present principal of that realm, and had been for many years. I therefore hazarded, rightly, that Mrs. Gresham had ruled her domain since the time of Mr. Stevens. As to the last, Sarah, she never referred to you as other than ' Mrs. Colethorpe', thereby clearly indicating her loyalties.'

" Truly remarkable, Holmes,' I told him, marvelling once more at the skill with which he read the minds of those about him with the same ease as that with which he traced footprints in muddy ground.

" It is nothing," waving a deprecatory hand. " I have

reason to believe, Madame, that the recent events were instigated by your present husband."

Mme. Montpensier started in surprise. " So that note that was found was true ? The wretch has been skulking around this house and terrifying my poor Annabel ? "

" By no means. He would not expose himself to such a risk. His foul schemes were carried out with the aid of his creature, the kitchen-maid Sarah."

" And the meaning of the note ? " I wondered aloud. " What is meant by that ? "

" Later, Watson. For now, Madame, I would like your permission to send for Sarah and for me to search her room."

" Certainly you may, though I have no idea what you expect to find there."

" I have my ideas," Holmes remarked grimly. " Watson, I will require you to prevent Sarah from entering the room while I am searching it, or leaving the house, as I fear she may attempt to do if she learns of what I am doing."

" Very well," I replied, though I was unsure how to best accomplish the task.

Holmes left the room and we heard his tread as he ascended the stairs.

" I think we had best call for Sarah and keep her in this room," said Mme. Montpensier, a suggestion to which I readily assented. She rang the bell, and requested Hannah, who answered, to send Sarah Nolan to us.

In two or three minutes, the kitchen-maid entered, a sullen look on her face.

" Yes, madam ? " she said, with an air that bordered on insolence.

" You are to stay here and not leave the room until you are given permission," answered her mistress.

The girl took on a sulky expression and looked around her. " Where's the other two gentlemen that were here ? " she asked, with more than a little aggression in her voice.

" One has returned to London, and the other is upstairs searching your room," I told her.

Immediately her face changed, and her mouth hung open. She said nothing, but suddenly turned quickly and made for the door. I was able to intercept her on the way, and stood between the door and her, barring her way. Her fists beat frantically against my chest before she raised her hands in an attempt to claw my face with her nails. I seized her by the wrists as she screamed such words as I never wish to hear again from the mouth of a woman.

" You have no right ! " was the general tenor of her remarks, though expressed in different words, over and over again. At length Mme. Montpensier rose from her seat, and delivered two stinging slaps to the girl's cheeks, upon which she ceased her ranting and allowed her arms to fall to her sides as she started to weep.

" You little wretch ! " Mme. Montpensier addressed her. " How dare you worm your way into this house, you poisonous serpent ? "

Through her tears, Sarah responded, " It wasn't what was meant to happen, madam. Forgive me ! Please forgive me ! "

" That, I think, will be a matter for the judge and jury at your trial, Sarah," replied Holmes, entering the room. " Madame, if you would ring for Hannah and send her to the police to take this woman," with a nod to Sarah, " into custody, I would be much obliged." He reached in his pocket, and held out a small morocco-bound notebook. " Where did you get this ? " he demanded of the kitchen-maid.

" That is Annabel's memorandum book ! " cried Mme. Montpensier. " It was a gift to her from me three years ago. How did you come by it, Sarah ? "

There was no answer, as the girl stood sullenly, her eyes on the floor, repeating at intervals, " Forgive me".

" It is of course your step-daughter's," Holmes answered himself. " I discovered it secreted under the mattress in Sarah's room. I took the liberty of leafing through the pages, and I discovered what I expected to find. Watson, pray make notes of this conversation. They may prove to be evidence in the trial."

" What exactly did you expect to find, Mr. Holmes ? "

" The draft of a novel, or rather a short work of fiction, written by your daughter. I am no great judge of literature, but it seemed to me that it was not well-written, I am afraid. However, there was one page missing. A page in which the heroine describes her fear of death resulting from poison, and her terror concerning a man outside her window. That page had been removed with a pair of nail-scissors. Sarah, can you read ? "

Our eyes turned to Sarah, who had turned pale. " Yes, sir," she whispered. " I was taught how to read and write at the orphanage."

" And who told you about this little book ? "

" It was Mr. Colethorpe told me, sir."

" Did he mention how it was that Miss Stevens came to be writing in this book ? "

" No, sir, he did not. All he told me is that there was a book in Miss Annabel's desk, and what it looked like."

" When did you remove it from her desk ? "

" About three months ago, sir."

" I remember. About that time, Annabel was distracted and somewhat distraught," said Mme. Montpensier. " She had lost something, but she refused to tell me what it was that had gone astray."

" Perhaps she was embarrassed about her writing. I believe this is often the case with young authors," Holmes explained. " Though there is nothing that I have seen here that appears overly personal, it may be that she felt that she had revealed too much of herself in these pages."

" You knew this book was in Sarah's room ? "

" I did not know of a certainty, but I had my suspicions."

" But how did you know that it was there, and that it had not been written on that fateful night ? "

" Remember the appearance of the desk earlier, Watson. Can you recall what was there ? Remember that the page in question was written in blue-black ink."

" I remember."

" Remember also that there was no such ink as that in the desk. There was black ink and red ink, but no blue-black ink. Also, you will note that there were no steel-nibbed pens in the desk, such as were used to write in the notebook, only fountain pens. Hence my remark to you, which you considered mysterious at the time, regarding the eating of soup with a fork. Why would anyone deliberately choose a clumsy and inefficient method of writing when a more convenient one was to hand ? The use of a steel-nibbed pen to write the piece was presumably a deliberate affectation, as was the use of the blue-black ink, and made me believe that there was something of the artistic temperament at work. From my knowledge of this type of mind, I may reasonably conclude that having lost the manuscript of her oeuvre, Miss Stevens thereupon removed all memory of the means used to produce it—that is to say, the pens and the ink. At any event, we may be certain that the paper found on the desk was not written on the night that Miss Stevens met her untimely end. When did you put it there, Sarah ? "

" When I got up in the morning, before anyone else was awake."

" And the rat poison in the sugar container which you substituted ? "

Sarah looked at him, obviously astounded at Holmes' deduction, but made no comment, simply replying to his question. " Just that evening, sir. I had the other jar in my room all ready. Mr. Colethorpe had given it to me the last time he stayed here. It was easy enough for me to change them over when Cook's back was turned, and to slip upstairs and hide the other one in Mrs. Colethorpe's room." She stared at Mme. Montpensier with a look that spoke of poisonous hatred, for which I could not divine the cause.

" You were aided in this by two things, were you not ? The first being the indisposition of Mrs. Gresham that night, allowing you undisturbed access to the kitchen. The second was the fact that your mistress elected on that night to prepare the drink herself. How did you know that it would be on that night that she would prepare the cocoa ? "

" I did not. Since Miss Annabel was feeling unwell that evening, though, it seemed to me that that evening she would make the cocoa, as she had done before when

Miss Annabel was in that kind of state. There had been other occasions when I had guessed that she would make the cocoa, but this was the first time that I had changed the jar and she had actually done it."

We were interrupted by a knock at the door, and a member of the local constabulary entered, escorted by the faithful Hannah.

" Ah, Sergeant," Holmes said to him. " My name is Sherlock Holmes. You may have heard my name ? "

" Indeed I have, sir. May I help you ? "

" Indeed you may, and you will be helping your own career if you do so by arresting this young lady and taking her to the station."

" Indeed, sir ? " said the stolid defender of the law, looking at the obviously terrified Sarah. " On what charge ? "

" On the charge of the murder of Miss Annabel Stevens," said Holmes. " There may be other charges pertaining to conspiracy to pervert justice and so on, but murder will suffice for now."

" Very good, sir," answered the policeman, obviously somewhat taken aback. " This is the one what did it, then ? I'm very glad that that's all cleared up."

" One more thing, Sergeant. When you return to the station, contact Inspector Lestrade at Scotland Yard and inform him of the arrest. He will no doubt wish to come here and take charge."

" Don't let them send me to prison, madam ! " shrieked the kitchen-maid, as the constable led her away.

" I will gladly see you hanged for your foul deeds," replied her mistress. " And I hope that your soul burns in hellfire for evermore ! "

With these words, she slammed the door on the departing policeman and his charge and turned to us.

" I apologise for my outburst just now," she said. " I cannot conceive of how such a one as that came to be so wicked."

" Love," stated Holmes. " Love of one even more wicked than she. A powerful and destructive force."

" Love of whom ? "

" Of your husband, Mr. Ferdinand Colethorpe. I had guessed some time ago from your description of his habits and actions that this was not his only household. He has been maintaining another wife and possibly a family for some time now, I am sure. His marriage to you was, I am sorry to say, more the result of attraction to your late husband's money than of his attraction to your personal charms. When he discovered the terms of Mr. Stevens' will, he realised that the obstacle to his future wealth was your step-daughter, who had to be eliminated if he was to gain financially.

You told me earlier that Sarah was previously his servant. My guess, which I am certain will be confirmed when the police question him, is that he had at some time, and possibly still is, in her eyes at least, Sarah's lover."

" My God ! Can such a man be suffered to walk this earth ? " burst out Mme Montpensier.

" It is quite likely that he had promised her not only his love, but a share of the money he imagined he would acquire on your step-daughter's death. In any case, he had planned thoroughly. The poison was to be administered by your hand—forgive me, Madame," he said gently as Mme. Montpensier broke into a fresh fit of weeping. " He would be safely away from the house, none to know where, and he would be free of any suspicion."

" The page from the notebook ? "

" We may assume that he came across this literary effort as the result of searching the desk. Seeing the passage, he realised that it would fit his plan perfectly. It may be, on the other hand, that he refined his plan as a result of reading that passage. In any event, it was perfectly suited for his needs. Sarah, being able to read and write, could be trusted to steal the correct memorandum book, and to locate the correct passage, remove it, and keep it until it was needed to provide a masterful piece of misdirection."

Holmes' deductions were soon proven to be correct when he and I made our way back to London and called in at the police station where Colethorpe, or Richards, to give him his proper name, was being interviewed by Lestrade.

" What a pitiful shrimp of a man he is, to be sure," remarked Holmes as an aside to me when we first saw him, and indeed, it was hard to determine how the small pink-faced man with his thin sandy hair had managed to engage the affections and trust of Mme. Montpensier. He spoke in a pitiful whine as he answered the questions that Lestrade and Holmes put to him, confirming the evidence that I had recorded during Holmes' interrogation of Sarah, showing little remorse at the relation of his deeds with which he was confronted.

As had been foretold, Richards was married to another,

and had lived at Holborn with his family for the past ten years. A firm of lawyers with which he had been employed in the past had had dealings with the late Mr. Stevens, and it was from this source that he had learned of the latter's wealth, and his demise.

He had therefore determined to take on a new identity and woo the widow, for whom, it appeared, he had or no feeling whatsoever, his affections being chiefly tied to the lawful Mrs. Richards and her children.

He had, however, found some place in the heart of the kitchen-maid Sarah, whom he had persuaded to leave her post with the family for who she was working, a neighbour of the Richards family, and take up a position in the new household into which he had married. Once she was in place, he proceeded to lure her with promises of leaving both his existing wives, and setting up a new existence with her in Canada, using the money that he was sure would come to him, following the decease of Miss Annabel Stevens, and the arrest and conviction of her step-mother.

He had somehow managed to discover the story that Annabel Stevens had been secretly writing in her memorandum book, and had noted a passage there where the heroine was describing her fear of her impending death. Whether he had his diabolical scheme already in his head, or whether he was inspired by this, he refused to say, but he had instructed Sarah to purloin the book at a suitable opportunity. The cunning of his whole plan, as Sherlock Holmes pointed out to me later, was that at all critical junctures, he was away from the house with an unshakeable alibi, while his unsuspected cat's-paw set the snare.

The rat poison was found in the household, as

Lestrade had foretold, having been purchased for its proper purpose. The only missing part of his plan was a duplicate sugar container, which he purchased and gave secretly to the kitchen-maid, instructing her to place only a thin layer of the poison over the top of the sugar after exchanging the jars, in order to make the introduction of poison into the food or drink by Mme. Montpensier, whichever presented itself as an opportunity, appear deliberate, rather than as an accident occasioned by the inadvertent substitution of rat poison for sugar.

He and Sarah Nolan were remanded for the Assizes, where eventually they were found guilty of the various crimes against them. Before that time, though, I asked Sherlock Holmes, " Why did you decide it was not suicide ? "

" I knew as soon as I had seen the note discovered in the dead girl's room. It was a case of the signature at the bottom of the note."

I cast my mind back. " There was no signature, Holmes," I pointed out.

" Precisely. Every suicide note I have ever encountered personally or of which I have heard reports has been signed by the writer. A suicide note is a final act of personal will—the most desperate act that any human being can accomplish—and we wish our names to be associated with such acts."

" And the innocence of Mme. Montpensier ? "

" I was positive of it when she came to collect her pince-nez that time. You remember that I had deduced that she played the viola, but it transpired that she played the violin ? When she visited, I invited her to play on my Stradivarius. She did so, with such an elegance of tone, and such deep feeling for the music, which was the solo from the second movement of Chaikoffski's violin concerto in D major, that I felt convinced that a woman with such a soul could never willingly harm another. It is, as you know, one of the most haunting pieces in the repertoire, and she played it from a depth of pure passion that reached to the bottom of my heart."

" Really, Holmes," I could not forbear from laughing. " This is most unlike your usual rational self."

" Believe me, Watson," he answered me with an expression of gravity on his face. " I was never more serious in my life. Though artifice may hide a black soul, true art can never do so, and when she played to me, I knew I was in the presence of true art. True in every sense of the word, that is."

Such was the affair of Mme. Montpensier, where the stern rationality of Sherlock Holmes gave way to a depth of feeling that it was hard to credit, even to me, who knew him as well as any man alive, and should give the lie to any who claim he was nothing more than a cold heartless reasoning machine.

The History of
John Augustus Edward Clay
As Told by Himself*

---

*   Editor's note: this is the title as given in the original manuscript.

Editor's notes

This packet of papers that I discovered in the second box of Dr Watson presented me with the biggest surprise so far in my researches. The paper itself was of a coarse nature, and of a size completely different from any other documents in the box. The handwriting was neither that of Dr. Watson nor of Sherlock Holmes, and was in a neat, somewhat crabbed hand. Pinned to the back of the sheaf of papers were a few pages in the now familiar writing of John Watson. As I read these, I became aware that I held in my hands the story of the notorious John Clay, whose exploits with regard to the Red-Headed League have been so vividly described.

I was, however, at a loss to explain how these memoirs of a confessed criminal came to be in the possession of Dr. Watson, an intimate friend of an upholder of the law, indeed, one who had actually been responsible for the arrest and incarceration of the author of these memoirs. Intrigued, I read on as Watson explains how he came to be in contact with John Clay, and the reasons for the inclusion of this manuscript with his accounts of the cases of Sherlock Holmes. At intervals throughout the manuscript, I came across notes on scraps of paper pinned to the original story. These were in the handwriting of John Watson, and I have included these as footnotes. I have also added some of my own notes where I feel that some additional explanation is needed.

I therefore make no apology for the inclusion of this document alongside Watson's accounts of the adventures of Sherlock Holmes. To see one of the most famous cases of

Sherlock Holmes " from the other side" is indeed a fascinating experience, and one which I feel will be of great interest to all students of the great detective and his methods.

Ladies and gentlemen, I give you Dr. Watson's introduction to John Clay's account of his life and exploits, followed by the story of the " fourth smartest man in London" in his own words.

DR WATSON'S INTRODUCTION

FOLLOWING THE ADVENTURE of Sherlock Holmes which I have described in *The Red-Headed League*, John Clay and his accomplice were sent for trial at the Assizes, Clay receiving an extended sentence of penal servitude and his confederate receiving a lesser punishment. I had been somewhat impressed, despite my initial feelings toward him, by the demeanour of John Clay during his apprehension by the authorities, and felt that, while his sentence was deserved, there was a good chance that this young man of obvious good breeding and intelligence could nonetheless become a useful member of our society at some time in the future.

When I mentioned this to Sherlock Holmes, he scoffed at my pretensions.

" I am afraid, Watson, that you take far too optimistic a view of human nature. As I mentioned earlier to you, I have had many skirmishes with Clay in the past.

None of his actions has been in any way able to persuade me that he is anything other than a thoroughgoing villain who will never change his ways."

I failed to be convinced by Holmes's arguments. In John Clay's appearance and general deportment I was reminded of a subaltern in my former regiment, who had behaved despicably and dishonourably on a number of occasions. Following some disciplinary action and subsequent light punishment for his offences, he became a model officer, and rapidly gained deserved promotion. I felt that with suitable encouragement, John Clay might also achieve similar redemption.

Without the knowledge of Sherlock Holmes, I made the journey to Pentonville prison and made a request to interview Clay, which was rapidly granted, chiefly on account of my association with Holmes. Naturally, given the circumstances of our previous meeting, he regarded my visit with a good deal of suspicion, and could not at first comprehend the reason for my visit. Eventually, I was able to convince him of my good intentions towards him, and he began to speak of his early life and of some of his criminal exploits. Having viewed the criminal life of London from one side, that of Sherlock Holmes and the police, it was extremely interesting for me to listen to an account from the other side, as it were. He spoke in an educated fluent voice, totally unlike that which he had used in his character of Vincent Spaulding, the pawnbroker's clerk.

My interest obviously communicated itself to him, and he requested that I visit him once again a week later.

" I have a scheme in mind which I think will be of interest to you," he said to me. Noting the expression of distrust on my face, he went on, " It is all legal. There is no need for you to pull that sort of face as if I'm asking you to rob a bank. I've had an interesting life, as some might say, and I think it could be an idea if I were to set down some of the features in it. You're a literary kind of gentleman, as we know. Maybe you could approach a publisher and let the world know about John Clay."

I was unsure of the morality of such a course of action, but I admit to having been intrigued by his proposal. " Very good, then," I said to him. " If you can write the first few pages of your story, I can at the very least look them over and let you know if there may be a suitable market for them."

Accordingly, I made arrangements with the prison governor for a visit at the same time the following week. On my keeping the appointment, Clay showed me some pages of his writing, which form the first few pages of the attached manuscript. I read them through and realised that they formed an interesting and important document, albeit one which, in my opinion, no responsible publisher could ever consider releasing to the public.

I told Clay as much, and his face fell. " D___ the hypocritical morality in this country ! " he cried. " Why should I not be allowed to talk to the world with the same sort of voice as your precious Sherlock Holmes ? "

I informed him that it was not so much a matter of morality, as of pure necessity on the part of the publishers, who would face prosecution if they released these words,* but I fear that I failed to convince him of this. Nonetheless, he informed me that he found some release from the strains of his current circumstances in

---

* Editor's note: It is doubtful if they would have faced prosecution. It seems that Watson was indeed applying his own morality here, and seeking justification.

setting down the facts of his life, telling me that he intended to continue with his history and would present it to me when it was finished. He implored me to attempt to find a public market for it, even though I continued to insist that such a course of action would almost undoubtedly result in failure.

I left him, not at all convinced that he would have the application and persistence necessary to complete his task, but I was pleasantly surprised when three months later I received a message in his own hand inviting me to make a further application to visit him.

" I am done with the project which we discussed some months ago," the note informed me. " I would be obliged if you would call upon me at my present residence, circumstances making it difficult for me to visit you at yours." The whimsical humour and resignation to his fate displayed here, coupled with my natural interest and curiosity to see what he had written, made it impossible for me to refuse his invitation. Accordingly, the next week saw me in Pentonville prison once more, talking to John Clay.

" It's all here," he told me, handing over a packet of neatly written papers. " Now, Dr. Watson, you may not consider me as a friend, but I am sure that you realise by now that I am by no means the desperate villain and unrepentant thief that your account of me has made me out to be. I do have some contact with the outside world, you know, and I saw your wonderfully dramatic relation of the events that put me here as published in the *Strand Magazine*. I have given my account of this little adventure here, along with some others in which your friend also played a part, even though we actually met for the first time on that fateful day in Saxe-Coburg-square." I accepted his manuscript with thanks, and he continued, " I remember what you told me about the impossibility of these little exploits ever reaching the public eye. I would ask you, though, to make every effort to set the record straight." He paused to cough into a handkerchief. I noted spots of blood on the cloth, and I started.

" Yes, Doctor," he said to me. " The climate in these lodgings is not of the most salubrious. I fear it is consumption, and the prison doctor has recently confirmed this to me. I probably have not more than a few months left to live, and you need have no fear that by helping to publish my words you are giving comfort and assistance to a desperate criminal, as I will no longer be on this earth."

Naturally, my pity was aroused by this circumstance, and I gave him every assurance that I would attempt to honour his wishes. In the event, however, although I made approaches to my publisher and to the *Strand Magazine*, I was unable to achieve his desired goal of publication. Many indeed expressed their interest, but it was as I had feared. The nature of the writer and of the subject matter made it impossible for them to make the material available to the public.

Within a few months of my last meeting with John Clay, I received a message from the governor of the prison that the prisoner had indeed succumbed to the disease in the prison infirmary, and that his body now lay in the graveyard of the penitentiary. Having received no clear instructions from Clay regarding the disposition of his manuscript, I forbore from any further attempts at publication, and locked it away. The time has now come for me to deposit some of my untold cases of Sherlock

Holmes in a safe location, and it occurs to me that this extraordinary story should be retained alongside those cases of my famous friend, seeing that it bears so closely on, and is at times so closely intertwined with, the adventures of the great detective.

John Clay speaks 1: The Professor

First, I would like to set the record straight. In Dr Watson's account of the little adventure that placed me in the predicament in which I now find myself—that is, incarcerated in Pentonville prison—he records the words of one of the Scotland Yard detectives who claimed to have been on my trail for some time. Inspector Peter Jones refers to me as " John Clay, the murderer, thief, smasher and forger". Thief I may be, smasher I have been, and forgery is one of the crimes to which I plead guilty, but I am not a murderer. I have never taken the life of a fellow human being, nor have I ever attempted to do so. That particular crime is one of which I am guiltless, and I regard the words of Inspector Jones as a foul slander upon my name*.

That little affair of the Red-Headed League was, I may rightly be proud to say, one of my better notions,

---

* Editor's note: One wonders how Jones could have associated Clay with murder, if this account here is accurate. It was, of course, in Clay's interests to present a sympathetic a portrait as possible to the public, but it is noteworthy that the indictments brought against him at his trial failed to include any crimes of violence, let alone murder.

but I will write about that in its due place. If it had not been for the intervention of Sherlock Holmes at that time, I would almost certainly now be a rich man, living a life of luxury, probably in the South of France or some climate more suitable to my constitution than this damp cold prison cell.

Inspector Jones was correct in some of his other points, however. My grandfather was indeed a Royal Duke, even though he was never married to my grandmother, who was nonetheless of good family. Despite the unfortunate encumbrance of my father, she managed to make a good marriage, though in her alliance with Henry Clay, a well-known manufacturer, her family considered that she had demeaned herself.

My childhood, you may be surprised to learn, was a happy one. I had the best of educations, and attended Eton College until the age of eighteen, whereupon I entered Christ Church, Oxford. At Eton and Oxford I started cultivating those acquaintances which have been of such value to me in my subsequent career. It must be said, though, that the antecedents of my father were sufficient barrier to prevent me entering the highest of circles with ease. I resented this, failing to understand at the time that, in today's society at least, accidents of birth count for more than do natural abilities. As to the latter, I proved to be abundantly endowed with intelligence.

To give you an example of this quality, I had almost considered composing this memoir in Latin verse, an accomplishment for which I won prizes at both Eton and Oxford. I could likewise have written it in French or Italian, languages in which I consider myself fluent, or even in the thieves' cant commonly use in the East

End of London among the criminal classes. However, I will write my history in what has come to be my natural manner of speaking. I do not pretend to have literary leanings, but will simply set things down in such a way to inform the world, in a style that all will understand.

Now we come to an interesting distinction. I have just referred to " the criminal classes". I have also admitted to being a criminal in the eyes of the law. Do I, then, consider my place as being a member of these classes ? The answer is in my mind that I am with these criminal classes, but not of them, in the same way that an officer in our Services is with his men but not of them. I hope that I make my meaning clear here.

My resentment against those whom I felt to be my natural inferiors, but preened themselves as my social superiors, increased during my time at Oxford. There was one of these, as rich as Croesus, whom I regarded as being a fowl ripe for the plucking. Lord Barrington, who was the descendant in the legitimate line of my ducal grandfather, ostentatiously flaunted his wealth and his social position. To me it was intolerable that this blockhead should enjoy all the privileges and enjoyment which seemed denied to me. I cultivated his friendship, naturally concealing the fact of our common grandfather, and rapidly became a regular attendant at his drinking parties and expeditions to the local houses of ill fame. I had many occasions to study his hand, and at night in my rooms I practised his signature and his writing. One day, while I was visiting him in his rooms, he had occasion to leave me alone there temporarily. I had previously remarked that he kept his cheque-book in an unlocked drawer of his desk, and I swiftly removed the last cheque, together with its counterfoil, from the back of the book. That evening, I wrote a cheque which was payable to " Cash" in the amount of £1000. I fully believed that his bank account was well able to withstand such a demand.

Alas ! I was unaware that on the day previous to my little deception he had withdrawn a large sum of money in order to place a bet on the 2000 Guineas running at Newmarket. His fancy had failed to win, or even to place, and he was accordingly temporarily out of pocket, with little money remaining in his bank account. When I presented the cheque at his bank in Broad Street, the matter was brought to his attention and he naturally denied ever having written such a cheque. It took little time for my guilt to be exposed, and as a result I am unable to claim the status of a graduate of the University of Oxford. Perhaps I should amend my words here. It is not so much that I am unable to claim the status of a graduate of the University, as that I am unable to claim such a status honestly. Indeed, my knowledge of the geography and the customs of the University has been of great value to me in my career. However, thanks to the wishes of the House to prevent scandal, and at the request of Lord Barrington, who seemed to retain a rather inexplicable affection for me, the police were not called in, and I was spared the complications of criminal proceedings.

My father, being of the amiably honest class of English tradesmen, was horrified at this setback to my career. He had, I believe, entertained some hopes that I would become ordained as a clergyman in the Church of England, a prospect which now fills me with some amusement, given my current circumstances. He now proposed to me that I take a post in his enterprise, with the eventual goal of taking over the business when he retired. However, I had no wish to spend my days at a desk surrounded by pens and paper. I therefore took myself off to France, where I spent six months among the Apaches of Paris, and a further half year in Naples, where I came into contact with some of the Camorra, the notorious Italian criminal society. I may say that my knowledge of English customs and society, not to mention my knowledge of the language, was of great value to the Neapolitan gangs with whom I associated, who were thereby able to relieve many wealthy English travellers of their money by a variety of tricks and ruses.

In this way, I was well able to support my adventures abroad. Those to whom I provided my aid were more than generous in providing me with a portion of the spoils. This provided me with the way in which I proposed to lead my life, at least for the next few years. However, I resolved that I would take no part in any crime of violence. Even when I was with the Parisian Apaches, I had refused to take part in any assaults against persons, and had confined my activities to informing my new colleagues regarding movements of my fellow countrymen, provided such information would not lead to any injury. I had likewise come to a similar agreement with the Neapolitan gangs. Such money as was taken from the English tourists there was taken by craft and stealth, rather than violence. Strangely enough, my French and Italian colleagues seemed to respect me for my preference, and saw it as the mark of an English gentleman.

You may put it down to a natural delicacy, or whatever you please, but the fact remains that I entertained, and retain to this day, a horror of causing harm to my fellow-man, for whatever reason. This prejudice has exposed me to the scorn of others, but I have resolutely continued to abide by these principles, inexplicable as they may seem.

By removing myself from the scene of the actual crime, I felt less likely to suffer the effects of the law should the worst come to the worst. I saw my future path as a supplier of information and intelligence to those who would perform the actual deed. This seemed to me to be an admirable way in which I could continue to exist, and hence I returned to London, armed with an introduction to one of the foremost organising criminals in that city, Professor James Moriarty.

I called at the address which I had been given, and left my card. I had seen no reason to use any name other than the one with which I was born. Indeed, if he wished to verify my antecedents—to take up references, if you will—he had only to make enquiries in Oxford, where he could verify that I was to be trusted in such matters as those in which he himself was involved.

The next day, I received an invitation to present myself for interview at a suburban address on the other side of London to that where I had left my card.

On arrival at the house, I was admitted by a servant, and found myself facing a man in whom I instantly recognised an intelligence that appeared at least equal to my own. I had made some enquiries before my visit, and I knew that the man before me had a reputation in the field of mathematics—a subject in which I had little ability and less interest. Even so, this man was not to be regarded lightly.

" How did you hear of my name ? " were his first words to me.

" I was given your name by Signor Gasparini in Naples."

The name of the famous leader of one of the largest gangs of the Camorra had its effect. " So you claim to know him ? " he asked me, his eyes burning. " Tell me the names of his two daughters."

" I never heard that he had any daughters," I answered him. " To the best of my knowledge he has three sons, named Antonio, Luigi, and Pietro."

" Very good, very good," he chuckled. " Of course, such information could be obtained by other means. Tell me, then, what you know of Lady Symington-Hopkins."

The lady in question was one of the English travellers to whom I have previously alluded, who had been relieved of the responsibility and cares associated with the ownership of a valuable diamond necklace during her stay in Naples. It was I who had informed Signor Gasparini and his men of her habits, intelligence which had allowed them to carry out the theft. I presented Professor Moriarty with all the information that I felt was relevant to the incident.

" Excellent," he replied. " Such information could only come from one who was party to this little adventure. Tell me more about yourself."

I proceeded to give him the outline of the facts that I have written above. He sat in his chair silently, unmoving, as I told my tale. When I had finished speaking, there was silence for a few minutes while he appeared to consider my words. At length, he spoke.

" And what is it that you propose to do for me ? "

I proceeded to outline my proposal, which was that I, being a personable and well-educated young man, could work my way into the fringes of society and thereby gain information which could be of use to Professor Moriarty's minions. I concluded by saying, " I realise that it is difficult for me to make demands of you, sir, but I would request that I not be involved in any incidents where violence is involved. I have a horror of such."

Moriarty raised his eyebrows. " I have never heard of such a thing," he exclaimed. " Do you really have such a delicate stomach regarding such matters ? "

" Sir," I explained, " I do indeed have scruples about such behaviour, and while I feel I am justified in relieving my fellow men of their material possessions, I do not feel that I have the same right to relieve them of their lives or of their health."

He threw back his head and laughed. " I find your scruples to be most amusing," he told me. " Very well, then. Of course you will require some compensation for your efforts, will you not ? What do you consider to be a suitable fee ? Would a tenth part of the proceeds seem appropriate ? "

" When I was working in Naples, I received fifteen per centum," I answered him, as coolly as I dared.

" Our Italian friends obviously reward genius well. However you can rest assured that the prices I am able to obtain as the results of your labours will be considerably in excess of those within the reach of Signor Gasparini. If you do your job well, I can promise you that you will be a very wealthy man indeed. Let me give you an assignment and I can then judge for myself the quality of your work. If it meets my demands, which I may tell you now are exacting, then maybe I can consider a figure higher than my original offer."

" Thank you, sir."

" There is, however, one further condition that I must

impose on you. While you are in my service, you are in my service alone. You must perform no work of this kind for any other person, or on your own account. I am your employer, and your efforts must be directed solely in the directions towards which I point you. I am a generous employer, and you may be sure that even if your work fails to bring in the revenue that I expect it to do, you will not be allowed to go penniless. Even the meanest of my employees, as long as he continues to work for me, and works to further my ends, deserves this. Note well, though, that failure to observe my rules, or any attempt at treachery, will inevitably result in your death. Rest assured of that last."

" And should I wish to terminate my employment with you ? "

" I do not see that as a very likely possibility, but let me explain how we would deal with that situation. Should you wish to cease your association with me, you will give me one month's notice, as is the standard practice. At the end of that month you will cease to work for me, and I will cease from issuing further orders to you. However, you should be aware that by leaving my employ, you do not cease to be under my scrutiny. My agents are everywhere, and you will be watched. Should you take it into your head to contact the police or any similar agency regarding me or my activities or those of my agents, or should you imagine that the skills and knowledge that you have gained through your association with me can be put to use on your own account, you will be killed."

He said these last words in a completely matter-of-fact tone that chilled me far more than if they had been uttered in anger or in a threatening tone of voice.

" I understand, sir."

" Good, I am pleased to hear it. So you are sure that you wish to work for me under these conditions ? "

" If I were to reply in the negative ? " I ventured.

" The same conditions would apply as those I have just described for those leaving my employ. You would be watched, and at the least sign of your attempting to contact the authorities, or of setting up in business on your own, you would cease to be. I hope that is clear ? "

" Perfectly clear. I accept your terms."

" Excellent. Welcome to my little organisation. For obvious reasons, there is to be no written contract between us, but you will find me a man of my word. As long as you continue to obey my instructions you will find that you will not want for anything. By the way, it is most unlikely that we will meet again. I always like to verify personally the quality of the higher members of my organisation, such as you will undoubtedly prove to be, but I find it to be less than convenient, or perhaps I should say that I feel more secure, if I keep future meetings to a minimum. As an intelligent man, I am sure that you understand this. A very good day to you, sir."

He rose, and without shaking hands, he turned and left the room. The servant who had admitted me appeared once more and showed me to the door. I had many questions to ask, but none to ask them of, and I left the house not a little perplexed and bewildered, but felt assured that I had secured some sort of future in the country of my birth.

John Clay speaks 2: The air-gun

In a short space of time, I found myself heavily involved with the execution of the tasks connected with Professor Moriarty's business. As he had told me, I hardly ever met him again in person, but typically received my instructions through the medium of a post office box rented in a false name, using a cipher to which I had been given the key in a meeting with a subordinate. The cipher was an ingenious one, of which I do not propose to give the details here. Suffice it to say that to the best of my knowledge, in the years in which I used this cipher, the authorities never managed to break the code.

On those rare occasions when personal contact was needed, the messenger was usually Colonel Sebastian Moran, a large heavyset man who managed to inspire respect through his physical presence alone. One day I received a message in the now familiar code inviting me to a meeting with him. On my arrival at the specified location—a bench beside the Serpentine in Hyde Park—Moran nodded familiarly to me as I sat down beside him.

" I know that you can speak French and Italian," he said to me. " How's your German ? "

" Maybe not fluent, at least as far as speaking it is concerned, but fair enough. I can read it with sufficient ease to understand the writings of Goethe in the original."

He snorted. " Hard enough to understand the blighter in translation. Got through two pages once, and gave it up. In any case, if your command of the language is that good, we wish you to make a little expedition to Germany," he went on. " There is no advantage to us if you are unduly modest regarding your linguistic abilities. Do not hide such lights under a bushel in the future."

I made some gesture to indicate my understanding, and he continued.

" I am confident that you will be able to manage our business when you meet Herr von Herder." I should mention that whenever Colonel Moran talked to me, he always use the word " we" when referring to the wishes of Professor Moriarty, as if he and Moriarty were as one in everything. I had my doubts, though, as to whether this was actually the case, and regarded it as being a mere affectation on his part.

" May I ask the nature of my errand ? "

" It is merely to collect a piece of machinery which is being made to our special order. Circumstances prohibit me from making the collection in person. I am needed here to attend to certain matters."

Naturally, I had no choice but to accept the " invitation". I caught the boat train from Victoria the next afternoon, and made my way from Ostend to Essen, where I lodged in a small but comfortable hotel, the expenses of which I knew would be recompensed by Moriarty. Indeed, the professor had kept his word as regarded money. My share of the proceeds of the robberies performed on the basis of the intelligence that I supplied remained at one-tenth of the total, but as he had told me, Moriarty was able to receive a higher price for the stolen goods than had been possible in Naples, and my income was correspondingly increased. I do not regard myself as being hopelessly addicted to material gain, unlike others of my new colleagues, and I was more than content with the one-tenth share that had been allotted to me, saving most of it, though naturally I did not use a bank for the purpose. As regards what the colonel always termed " operational expenses", I had no cause for complaint. If I ever had to travel on Moriarty's business, I almost invariably travelled in the first class of whatever transport I used, and the lodgings in which I stayed were of a similar high quality; the expenses for these always being paid promptly and without complaint.

The morning after my arrival in Essen, I made my way to the address that I had been given. On knocking at the door and giving my name, I was admitted by a servant into a workshop filled with lathes and other machinery, the purpose of many of which was completely unknown to me. My studies at Eton and Oxford had not prepared me for such mechanical skills.

Seated in a corner of the workshop sat a small wizened old man whose general appearance, and ugly wrinkled face especially, reminded me of the gnomes of legend, busy polishing a piece of metal of unfamiliar shape. As he turned his face in my direction, I noticed that he was wearing spectacles whose lenses were of dark smoked glass. He greeted me in German, and I answered him in the same language. He held out his hand in greeting, in my general direction, but not precisely directed towards me. With a start, it came to me that this mechanic was blind.

I extended my hand in response, and he grasped it with a firm grip. His hand was dry and rough, the result obviously of many hours of labour.

" Would you prefer that we speak English ? " he asked me, in fluent but accented English.

" If that is agreeable to you," I replied.

He chuckled. " I spent several years in England,

before circumstances forced me to leave. I knew too many things about certain people, and certain people knew too many things about me."

My time spent in the service of Moriarty, and my natural caution regarding such matters, had taught me not to enquire too deeply into such matters, and though my curiosity was aroused, I refrained from asking any more questions.

" So, you have come for Colonel Moran's little toy ? " he asked me.

I was unsurprised to learn that the name of Colonel Moran, rather than that of Professor Moriarty, was associated with this business. As I implied earlier, Moriarty preferred to hide in the shadows, allowing his minions, such as myself to take the risks with which he would sooner not have his name associated. " So I believe. Though he gave me no idea as to the nature of the machinery which I was to collect from you."

" Then let me show you. I believe you will find it amusing. Have the goodness to pass me a long package wrapped in oilskin that you will find on the third shelf above my head."

I was impressed by the accuracy with which he described an object which he was unable to see with his own eyes and passed down the package, marvelling at its weight.

" Open it," he commanded me.

On my unwrapping the bundle, I beheld a collection of metal parts, together with a long complex piece of machinery consisting of two cylinders, ingeniously fixed to each other side-by-side. I must have made some noise of astonishment or puzzlement, because von Herder started to laugh softly. " I can tell that you have no idea in your head what it is that I have constructed for the colonel."

" I have not the faintest idea," I confessed. " If I were pressed for an opinion, I would say that it was a gun of some description, but I have never seen a gun like it." As it happens, my acquaintance with firearms was slim, so to confess my unfamiliarity hardly reflected to my discredit, in my eyes.

" Then let me show you," he said. With dazzling speed, his hands moved to assemble the components of the mechanism until it took on the appearance of a rifle, albeit one of a somewhat unfamiliar shape. All the while, his blind eyes appeared to be fixed on my face, a circumstance which I found to be more than a little unnerving. Finally his hands stopped moving and he parted his lips in a grim smile of satisfaction. " Here you are," he invited, extending the weapon towards me.

" I am still in the dark," I told him.

" The colonel has told you nothing of this, I can tell," he replied. " I do not perceive it will do any harm if I inform you of the purpose of this work that I have completed, which is some of the finest that I have ever produced. This, sir, is indeed a gun. A very special gun for a very special purpose. Firstly, allow me to point out that it is an air-gun. The advantage of an air-gun is that it may be fired, even in the middle of a crowd, or in a busy thoroughfare, without attracting undue attention. Its operation is nearly silent. In addition, I would like you to examine the barrel of this gun."

I did so, and remarked, " I am not familiar with weapons of this type, but it seems to me that this barrel is wider–I believe the term is ' of larger calibre'–than that usually employed in air-guns."

" Indeed it is. It is of the calibre usually associated with revolvers. And here," as his hands reached for a small box lying on his workbench, " are the bullets intended for it."

I opened the box, to reveal about fifty leaden bullets lying in a cushion of cotton wool. Though, as I say, I am not overly familiar with firearms, my observations allowed me to deduce that these were replicas of such bullets as are typically used in pistols. Naturally, there were no cartridges.

" You see now the beauty of this," continued the hideous little gnome beside me, patting the stock of the gun affectionately. " An almost silent weapon, whose bullets will expand on impact, and the sound of whose report will remain unheard, even in the midst of the most crowded metropolis."

I was horrified by the diabolical simplicity of this device. " Who is the intended target of this weapon ? " I asked.

" That, my dear sir, is not my concern," he told me. " It is enough for me to do my work well and receive payment for it. But before I receive my payment for my labours—and I trust that you have the money with you—I wish you to try my craftsmanship for yourself."

It was true that concealed in my breast pocket was a large envelope which Colonel Moran had presented to me in London, telling me that it was filled with Bank of England notes to be presented to von Herder on receipt of the " machinery". He had mentioned nothing, however, regarding the testing of the apparatus. How could he have done so, I asked myself, given that I knew nothing of its nature.

" I have no skill at these matters," I protested.

" Never mind, I am sure that the colonel will be pleased to hear from your own lips that his money has not been wasted. Come." He stood, handing the gun and the box of bullets to me, and made his way to a small door in the rear of the workshop. He opened it, and ushered me through into the back garden of his house. Some fifty yards away stood a small artist's easel, on which was a paper target some three feet in diameter.

I could claim almost no skill with firearms, and I had no experience whatsoever with a rifle such as the one which was now in my hands. However, it seemed pointless for me to resist the invitation.

" How do I operate this ? " I asked. The answer proved to be complex and surprisingly strenuous, involving levers and springs to pump up the air pressure in the chamber, which would then be released to propel the bullet towards its target. I lifted the weapon to my shoulder and steadied my aim as I squinted over the sights towards the square of paper with the black circle in its centre. Gently, I squeezed the trigger, prepared for the kick of the butt against my shoulder as I fired. Instinctively, I closed my eyes against the noise of the explosion, but there was no such sound. A peculiar mechanical sound with virtually no recoil was the result.

" Did you hit it ? " von Herder asked me excitedly.

" I cannot tell from here. I will examine the target." I walked the length of the garden, and was amazed to see that my shot had not only hit the target, but was close to the centre. I reported the result to the blind mechanic, who merely nodded in approval.

" So now that you know that it works, I receive my money, yes ? "

" First you must show me once again how to assemble

and disassemble this mechanism. I hardly feel that I can travel back to England carrying this in its present state."

I had been impressed by the ingenious nature of the weapon, and the workmanship with which it had been produced. I was struck with further admiration for the twisted ingenuity of the little gnome when we returned to the workshop, and von Herder revealed to me the secret methods by which it could be taken to pieces and put back together again. In its disassembled state, the smaller pieces fitted neatly into a small hand case, specially prepared with compartments for each component of the machine. The barrel and the air cylinder underneath it were disguised as the shaft of a rolled umbrella.

Despite my revulsion, I was impressed by these thorough preparations for the transportation of this infernal machine, and I complimented the German on his attention to detail. I handed over the envelope to him.

" Of course," he smiled, " I can count these pieces of paper with my fingers, but I am unable to tell if they are genuine Bank of England notes. You will forgive me, I am sure, if I call my assistant to verify that the colonel is indeed a man of his word."

" That would seem to be a natural precaution."

His fingers moved to an electric button on his workbench, which he pressed. About two minutes later, the door through which I had first entered opened, and a young lady entered.

" Helga, my dear," he said to her in German. " This young gentleman from England has been good enough to provide me with certain pieces of paper here in this envelope. Would you be kind enough to examine them and tell me what they are ? "

The young woman, whom I now perceived to be of considerable beauty, conforming to the German type, took the envelope and extracted the banknotes. She examined them with the air of an expert familiar with such matters, running the edge of her nail over the engraving, slightly wetting her finger and rubbing it over part of the cashier's signature, and holding the paper to the light to examine watermark.

At one point in the proceedings, her eyes met mine, and there was a look of what appeared to be pity in them. She said nothing to me, but merely reported, " All twenty of these Bank of England notes for fifty English pounds each appear to be genuine, Father."

" Very good, my dear. Maybe you can offer this young Englishman some refreshment before you send him on his way ? " He turned towards me. " Good day to you, sir," he added in English. " I have already forgotten your name, if ever I knew it, that is, and I pray that you will do me the same courtesy." He extended his hand, and I shook it, though with a certain distaste based on what I now knew of this man and his foul trade.

" Come," invited his daughter. " May I offer you some coffee before you depart ? " I accepted gladly, and left this diabolical workshop, which had filled me with horror since I discovered the purpose of the machinery which I had collected, meanwhile grasping the same machinery in its disguise of an innocent case and an umbrella.

You may call me a coward and a hypocrite for my actions. I must repeat that I am opposed to the use of violence in my operations, and yet here I was holding a device whose only purpose was the murder of other human beings. But I ask you to consider the fact that should I fail to execute the commission which had been entrusted to me, I knew that I would certainly fall victim to the wrath of Professor Moriarty. Even in my relatively short acquaintance with his organisation, I knew of three deaths within the group which could be laid at his door: two of those who had decided to carry out operations on their own account, and one of whom was reportedly a police spy. By throwing in my lot with the professor, I was now fully committed, and I no longer possessed free will as regards the actions I performed.

I was led into what I took to be a drawing-room, rather over-furnished in the German style, and my fair guide rang the bell to give orders for coffee and cakes to the servant who appeared. While we were waiting for the refreshments to be brought, she spoke to me.

" You seem to me to be a good man," she told me. " Why are you involved in this dreadful business ? "

" You know what your father is doing, then ? " I asked her in return.

" Of course I know, and I am powerless to stop him. How could I ever report my own father to the police ? Ever since he was forced to leave England on account of the scandal, he has been unable to find any work for his hands other than the kind of work he has just sold to you."

" If it is any consolation to you," I told her, " this here is not for my own use. I am merely the messenger who fetches and carries, not the man for whose use this is intended." I said this in German, unsure of whether I had expressed my meaning clearly, but her posture seemed to relax a little, indicating that I had probably conveyed successfully what I wished to impart. The coffee arrived, together with some small cakes, and we ate and drank in near silence. Eventually I rose to go.

" Many thanks for your hospitality," I told her. " I agree with you, that this is a dreadful business in which I find myself, but believe me, I have little or no choice in the matter." I looked into her eyes, and what I saw there impelled me to take her in my arms and draw her towards me. " Helga," I said to her, using the name by which I had heard her father address her. " We do not know each other, and we may never see each other again in this life. Believe me, though, I will never forget you." With these words, I kissed her on the lips, and she responded to my caresses.

" Enough ! " she told me at length, pushing me away. " As you say, we will never see each other again, and this is mere foolishness." I released her from my grasp with some reluctance, and stepped away.

" If you change your mind, Helga, and decide that you wish to meet me again, I am sure that your father can let you know how you may make contact with me. As for me, I shall respect your wishes, and not force my company on you further. Rest assured that it will be a long time, if ever, before I forget you."

So saying, I left her, and made my way to the railway station, to return to England at the earliest possible opportunity. My time on the trains and the boat carrying me back home was spent in reflection, of the strange perverted genius of von Herder, and the powerful attraction which his daughter had exerted on me.

I delivered the deadly weapon to Colonel Moran, who professed himself delighted with my work. His satisfaction showed itself later in an unmarked envelope, containing a considerable sum of money, which appeared through my letterbox one morning about a week later.

For some time after this little adventure I scanned the newspapers, searching for details of a death which appeared to have been caused by a revolver, but where no weapon had been found, and the sound of the fatal shot had not been reported.* However, there were no such reports, and my conscience remained relatively clear.

JOHN CLAY SPEAKS 3: THE ACID

FOLLOWING THE ADVENTURE in Germany that I have just described, it appeared that I had achieved some sort of measure of respectability in the eyes of Professor Moriarty and those who executed his orders.

One day, I was sent for by Colonel Moran, using the usual methods of communication as I described earlier. As always, I found myself to be more than a little afraid of this large, powerful, and I have no doubt, violent man as I stood before him.

" Sit down, sit down," he invited me, gesturing to the chair that stood on the opposite side of the table to

---

* Note in Dr. Watson's handwriting: " This gun, of course, was the one which was used by Colonel Moran in his murder of Ronald Adair and his attempted murder of Sherlock Holmes as I describe in *The Empty House*. There is also good reason to believe that it was employed in the case of the Trepoff murder, which I have also described elsewhere."

which he was standing. " There's no need for you to look so worried, you know. We are very pleased with the work you've been doing. There's another little job for you which is a bit different from what you've been doing up to now. The professor told me a little about your doings at Oxford. Have you kept your hand in with that sort of thing ? "

" By ' that sort of thing', you mean— ? "

" Oh, for God's sake, man. What do you think I mean ? I'm talking about the production of documents. Forgery, if you want it in plain simple English."

" I think my skills are as good as they ever were. After all, I have been using them to create messages from masters to servants for some time now, which have allowed houses to remain empty when they should have been occupied. I believe that given several pages of a person's handwriting—whether they be a man or a woman—I am able to compose at least a small message which would deceive even the writer him or herself."

" Excellent, I'm glad to hear that. The task to which I wish to assign you will bring more definite and larger rewards than the little notes you've been writing to decoy the servants away from the houses. We feel that you can help us produce IOUs which will bring in considerable sums of money." He proceeded to explain the scheme, which involved a number of confederates who would frequent gaming clubs and insert themselves into games where wealthy but inexperienced gamblers were taking part. Since such gamblers often imbibed heavily before commencing their games, often they had little or no memory of the previous evening when they awoke following the nights debauch. The plan was that the member of Moriarty's organisation who had taken part in the game would come up to the hapless gambler a few days afterwards, presenting an IOU in his own writing. If the victim protested his innocence, the gang member would then threaten to expose him as a man who was unwilling to pay his debts of honour. " It cannot fail," chuckled Moran. " After all, we will not be asking for large sums of money, but it will be enough to make the enterprise worthwhile, I can assure you. Naturally, you will share in the proceeds at the usual rate, and there will be plenty to go around."

I have to admit that the enterprise appealed to me. The victims would be those who could afford their losses, and they were of the class that had humiliated me in my early life. There was something very pleasing in the prospect of turning their own concepts of honour against them in this way.

" How do you propose that I obtain samples of their handwriting in order to produce the IOUs ? " I asked.

" We have our methods," he informed me. " Believe me, there are many servants who will be willing to provide suitable specimens for your analysis. We already have thirty targets in our sights."

The first of these (I do not propose to name names here—they are not really relevant to the story, but suffice it to say that they are all well-known names in politics and in society, and not one of them could in any way be described as being poor) was the second son of a famous peer of the realm who held a position in the Cabinet of the day. His valet had provided me, through a number of intermediaries, with letters that he had written and subsequently discarded. His hand was of the large illiterate variety affected by so many of our aristocratic " leaders", and was surprisingly easy to imitate.

I received a request in the usual coded form to produce a document promising to pay one " Henry Morton" the sum of £500. Naturally, I had no idea of the true identity of the debtor, nor the circumstances under which the debt was supposed to have been acquired. I produced the IOU as requested, and delivered it, through the medium of a post office box which had been rented for the occasion. Two days later, I found £50 in sovereigns delivered in a small package to my door. Moran sent for me the next day.

" You have done very well," he said, smiling his tiger-like smile. " Apparently our friend claimed to have no recollection of writing the IOU, but was convinced that it was indeed he who had written it. He blamed it, as we had expected, on the brandy and port that he had been drinking before and during the game. We will have another such opportunity for you within the week. In the meantime, we see a further opportunity for your talents in the form of bank cheques. There is a little more risk involved—though not for you, of course—but the pickings could be infinitely richer. After all, we have only a limited number of rich fools available to us, and only a certain number of clubs in which we can operate before we are spotted and from which we will be banned if our little game becomes apparent."

" This is definitely of interest. Can you give me a few more details ? "

" Certainly. We have a number of our people working in different banks throughout the City. We have arranged with them that when certain large corporations and enterprises draw on their accounts using cheques, these checks will not be cancelled the usual way through stamps or tearing off the corner as is usually the case, but will be sent on to us. Your job will be to use certain chemicals with which you will be provided, to erase the original payee and the amount payable, and to rewrite the cheque using the details which will be provided to you. The cheque will then be presented at a bank in a different part of the country. We anticipate that this will be a profitable business for us."

" Is that possible ? " I asked. " I was under the impression that erasing the writing on a cheque would cause the ink of the printed check form itself to be destroyed, showing that the cheque had been altered."

" You obviously underestimate the resources available to the professor. Thanks to his contacts in parts of Europe—regions in which I am glad that I will never have to set foot—he has been supplied with a small quantity of miraculous fluid which can erase the writing from cheques while leaving the underlying paper and the printing on it untouched*. We have been warned, though, that this fluid possesses highly corrosive properties. The scientist who supplied us strongly recommends the use of gloves when using it, and also to avoid inhalation of the fumes. I note that you are a sensible man and will regard these precautions with the respect that they deserve."

" When do you want me to start on this ? "

" The cheques will start to arrive in your box within

---

* Note in Dr. Watson's handwriting. " Sherlock Holmes, in the course of his chemical experiments, also discovered a liquid possessing similar properties, which he claimed would undermine the economic security of the nation's banking system were he to reveal it to the world. He accordingly destroyed the only sample, and the notes he had made describing the process leading to its production."

the week," he told me. " As to the fluid itself, it is here."
From his overcoat pocket the extracted a small wooden
box. " Within this box, surrounded by cotton padding,
lies a small bottle containing the mixture. You will be
the first in this country to use it. We cannot necessarily expect success at the first attempt, but of course, we
do not expect a large number of failures." So saying, he
passed the box to me, and I stowed it safely away in an
inside pocket. " I do trust that you will remember the
precautions I have told you," were his words to me on
parting.

As you can imagine, I was intrigued by the thought
of this seemingly magical chemical which could produce
large sums of wealth, seemingly out of thin air. I waited impatiently for the first of the checks to arrive in my
box. As Moran had told me, it was less than a week
before the message containing the cheque was in my
hands, together with the instructions as to how I was to
change it.

At my lodgings I had prepared a large sloping surface,
similar to that used by draughtsmen in drawing offices,
which stood under the window facing north. I considered this to be a perfect place for my work. I had not
opened the fatal box since it had been given to me, but
realised now was the time to do so.

I had previously purchased a pair of fine kid gloves,
which protected my hands, but still permitted sufficient freedom of movement and allowed my fingers to
feel the subtleties of the surfaces that they touched. I
drew these on, and prised open the lid of the box. Within, nestling in its padding of cotton waste, lay a small
bottle, with a label written in an alphabet which was not

ours, but which I recognised as the Cyrillic alphabet as used in Russia and neighbouring countries.

Carefully holding the bottle away from my body, I removed the stopper, releasing an acrid smell which made me cough. I set the bottle at some distance from me on the board and gingerly dipped the tip of the camel hair brush which I had previously purchased into the liquid. I applied this gingerly to the cheque, and was amazed to see the ink in which the amount had been written fade before my very eyes, leaving the printed ink completely untouched. I had no doubts regarding my ability to produce new words and figures corresponding to the instructions which I had been given, and so continued to apply the magical liquid to the cheque. I had nearly finished my work, which took not nearly the amount of time that I had expected, when there was a sudden knock at the door. I started, and temporarily forgetting that I held the brush in my hand, raised that hand to my face. The tip of the brush, still loaded with the mysterious liquid, touched my forehead, and I instantly experienced a burning sensation.

I started to emit a cry of pain, but realising that this would alert my visitor, managed to convert this into an enquiry as to who my visitor might be. Hurriedly replacing the stopper in the bottle and covering the cheque on which I had been working with a half finished sketch of a vase of flowers, which I had previously prepared for just such an occasion as this, I opened the door to my landlady, who was merely enquiring whether I would prefer cabbage or carrots with my boiled beef that evening. While we were conversing on this matter, I noticed her attention appeared to be fixed on my forehead, which was still experiencing a burning sensation.

When I had closed the door, I made my way to the washstand and gazed at my reflection in the mirror, where I beheld a white mark. I dashed water on my face, which relieved the burning sensation, but the white mark remained, and indeed remains to this day. I determined therefore to treat this liquid with more respect than I had hitherto done, and continued to alter the cheque in the way that had been demanded of me.

I delivered the cheque to a post office box in a large industrial city in the North of England. A week later I was sent for by Professor Moriarty himself. We met in a house in a district of London which I had never previously visited.

As opposed to his rather cold formal self that I had experienced on the previous occasion that we met, he now seemed affable. " Congratulations, Clay," he said to me. " Your latest work has indeed borne fruit, and there is absolutely no way in which any of it can be traced to us. This is an experiment which has well repaid any trouble we have taken in its preparation. I must warn you, though, that it would be advisable for you to change your lodgings."

" Why so ? " I asked in some perplexity. " If you say that this cannot be traced to us, surely I am in no danger from the police ? "

" You are completely right on both counts," he answered me. " However the danger in this case is not associated with your recent work, but with the IOUs that you recently produced so competently. It is not the police of which you need to be aware, but a private detective called Sherlock Holmes."

I must confess that the name of Sherlock Holmes being at that time unknown to me, I was unaware of his reputation or of his powers. I laughed. " I am sorry, Professor," I told him. " I have met several private detectives, and though they may enjoy some success in the finding of errant husbands or of straying poodles, I have yet to meet one whom I would consider in any way to be a foeman worthy of my steel."

Moriarty looked at me, shaking his head in that strange snakelike way of his. " I warn you, Clay, that you should not underestimate Mr Sherlock Holmes. He is more than a cut above the usual run of private detective. He would scorn the idea of tracing errant husbands or lost lapdogs with the same fervour that you would reject my suggestion that you steal apples from a costermonger's cart. He would regard the idea as being beneath his dignity and unworthy of his abilities. I confess that I would concur with him in this opinion. For from his being a foeman unworthy of your steel, he might well regard you as being unworthy of his. In order to guarantee your safety, I am sending you to the North, where I wish you to take up an identity for a few months which I guarantee will not be penetrated even by Sherlock Holmes. I am afraid I cannot promise you that it will be a comfortable existence. However, once we have thrown Mr Holmes off the scent, you may return to London, and I can assure you that your accommodation and conditions will be a substantial improvement on those you enjoy now, and we can resume our work on the cheques."

And so it was that I found myself tramping the vales of Northern Yorkshire in company with a band of Gypsies. As Moriarty had promised me, the life was uncomfortable, but the folk amongst whom I was living were friendly, and seemed to accept my presence. I have no doubt that gifts from Moriarty had smoothed my path. In my time with the Romanies I learned many things which were of subsequent value to me. I was taught the secret language of signs of stones and pebbles arranged in various ways for the benefit of those who might come after. I was instructed in the mysteries of the chalk marks that are to be found scribbled on garden walls and gates by those who travel the length and breadth of this country. I learned how to eat and drink when there was no food or drink apparently available. I even came to appreciate the finer points of Romany cuisine, including roasted hedgehog—a dish I can heartily recommend, by the way, although you will not find it on the menus of even the finest restaurants. One of the Gypsy women, hardly more than a girl, took a fancy to me, and I will confess that on the cold Yorkshire nights we often enjoyed each other's warmth. Although she knew that I was a bird of passage, she wished to see me as one of her own folk, and I submitted to the ceremony of having my ears pierced for earrings. Naturally, I have never worn these ornaments in London, but the holes in my ears, which I see in the mirror every morning as I shave, remind me of the girl I knew as Mary. I never did find out her true Romany name.

Though Moriarty had told me that I would be spending three months with the gypsies, the truth is that it was closer to four months before an emissary visited the encampment to seek me out and to inform me that in Moriarty's opinion it was now safe for me to return to London. I left my friends with some regret, and a deeper appreciation of their way of life. Indeed, if I had ever chosen to leave Moriarty's employ, it would have been to take up the wandering life with Mary, or one like her, together with her band.

On my return to London, I was installed, as had been promised, in superior lodgings in a fashionable quarter of London. I even had my own servants: a valet and a housekeeper to take care of my needs. Both of these were, naturally, in Moriarty's pay, and I felt there was no reason to conceal my general activities from them. However, following the advice given to me by Colonel Moran, I did not acquaint them with the details of my business. Even so, it was of great advantage to me in the assignments I was given which involved my participation in Society to have such a *pied-à-terre* available to me, complete with servants who could be trusted not to tell tales.

Many a Society beauty visited me, unknown to her husband or her lover, and while she lay in my arms told me secrets of her household—little details which she did not recognise as being secrets, but which proved to be of immense value to those of Moriarty's men who were later detailed to enter and to take the objects of value which she had described to me, and I had reported.

I began to believe that my work was of considerable worth to Moriarty and his organisation. Certainly I was well provided for, and I lacked for nothing. I even now had a certain place in the society which had hitherto rejected me, and I had no reservations about my chosen path.

JOHN CLAY SPEAKS 4: THE DARLINGTON BABY

I NOW WISH TO RELATE AN INCIDENT in which I was involved, where the true facts of the matter were never known to the public. Although I knew from others that Sherlock Holmes was involved, his part in the matter has never been described.* It occurred during the prosperous period of my life which I have described above.

It was not often that I received a visit from Colonel Moran, but he arrived unannounced at my door one day and was immediately shown into my drawing-room. Happily I was alone that afternoon. It would have been more than a little embarrassing for me and my *petite amie du jour* had he arrived some thirty minutes earlier.

" We have something a little out of the ordinary for you," were his first words to me.

I confess that I was a little worried by this. I was filled with the apprehension that these words might signify that I was to lose my current position in the organisation. " I may hope that my work has been satisfactory ? " I enquired.

" Absolutely, my dear fellow," he replied, with a hearty laugh. I was a little surprised by this joviality, which was far from typical of his usual temper. " In fact," he continued, " it is precisely because you have demonstrated your abilities in such a wide variety of fields that we have decided to use you in this coming operation. It

---

* As it happens, this incident was described by Watson, but was not revealed to the world until it was discovered, and published by Inknbeans Press as *The Darlington Substitution* in 2012.

demands a man of intelligence, which you have demonstrated in abundance over the past few months, as well as courage and daring, well mixed with the social skills that I hear you are demonstrating to a large number of admirers." He smirked unpleasantly at his last words, an expression which I chose to ignore.

" Enough of the flattery," I answered. This kind of praise was not typical of Moran, and I had a pre-sentiment that whatever was coming would be less than pleasant. My apprehension must have shown in my face.

" I am telling you nothing that we do not believe is the truth. This is a very delicate operation, and quite frankly, there is no one else that we can trust to do the work properly. You are acquainted with Elizabeth, Lady Hareby ? "

I was indeed well acquainted—in fact, " intimately acquainted" would be a better description of my relationship with the woman. Not that I had any reason to believe that I was the only one to enjoy her favours. She had made herself notorious in certain circles of society as a result of her antics. " Yes, indeed I am acquainted with her," I replied, as nonchalantly as I could manage.

" She has a little problem, and she wishes us to solve it," he informed me. " What do you know of her husband ? "

I have never met the man in question, and believed him to be a permanent invalid, following a fall sustained while hunting. There were many rumours about Town regarding his condition, and it was unclear whether his problem was a physical or a mental one. I informed Moran.

" Good, at least you have the background to the story.

Lady Elizabeth would like you to visit her, at her hotel, at six o'clock this evening. For reasons we need not go into, she is not staying at the Darlington town house. Can you see any reason why you should not be able to keep this appointment ? "

" There is nothing important that cannot be postponed," I answered.

" And when you last saw Lady Elizabeth, you parted on good terms, I take it ? " he persisted.

" Certainly there was no argument between us," I assured him. " I am sure that I will be welcome if I present myself."

" Excellent, excellent. How is your financial situation ? " he asked me, abruptly changing the subject.

I assured him that I had sufficient funds to meet any ordinary demand, and indeed could manage almost any unusual demands on my purse with little difficulty.

" This little caper may involve you in some considerable expense, and I wish to make sure in advance that you will have the funds available to meet any such outgoings. I am delighted to see that you possess your virtues of thrift and good housekeeping." He unleashed his tiger-like smile, before standing and letting himself out, pausing only to give me the name of Elizabeth Hareby's hotel.

At six that evening I was standing by the front desk of the luxurious hotel to which I have been directed, asking for Lady Hareby. A page led me to the suite in which she was staying, after first ascertaining that she was in a state ready to receive visitors.

I was admitted, much to the surprise of Elizabeth, who started when she recognised my face.

" John ! What are you doing here ? " she asked me.

" I am expecting someone else to arrive any minute now. I thought you were he, otherwise I would not have allowed you to visit me." She blushed, a little, possibly at the memory of some of our previous meetings.

" I believe that I am he whom you were expecting," I said to her. " You were expecting an individual to visit you at six o'clock, were you not ? I have been dispatched by a person whose name I will not mention, precisely for the purpose of visiting you here at six o'clock. For the moment you may assume that I am the person you are expecting. If anyone else makes an appearance then it may be possible that I am mistaken. I do not think this is likely, however."

" I had never suspected— When I talked to—"

" You do not need to mention names. In fact, let us avoid names in this conversation as far as is possible."

" I cannot believe that you are associated with these people, all the same," she protested. " When we were— Were you... ? "

" Yes, I was. You may rest assured, though, that I never took advantage of you in that way."

" But you took advantage of me in so many other ways," she giggled, in that mischievous manner that I remembered so well, and which still had the power to stir me.

" To business," I told her sternly, before the old Adam could assert itself within me.

" The truth of the matter is that I am ' in pig', as my younger sister would have it. You have probably heard that Edgar, my husband, is a helpless invalid in the family house up in Northumberland. Quite frankly, it cannot be expected that he will live for very much longer. And when he does, my child will inherit. I cannot inherit as his widow, because the estate is entailed."

" Surely his father, the Earl of Darlington, is still alive ? "

" The old fool cannot last much longer. When he dies and Edgar dies, the estate will pass to my child, as I say. That is on one condition."

" That condition being ? "

" That condition being that the child I bear will be male. If it is a female, the estate will pass to some distant cousin."

" But even if it is not a male child, surely the next child, or even the one after that may well be male and you will inherit the estate in a kind of regency ? "

She laughed bitterly. " Edgar is in no state to father any more children. And everyone knows this. Even if I were to have a child by another man, the world would know that it was not his child, and it would be disowned, and I would be cast out from the family. As it is, even though I assume that everybody knows of the little games I have been playing around Town, it is still within the bounds of possibility that I am carrying Edgar's child, and so everyone pretends that they know nothing of my amusements."

" What is it that I am to do ? " I was confused, being distracted by the proximity of this beautiful woman, and the scent that surrounded her.

" You are to ensure that the child will be male."

To say that I was taken aback would be an understatement. " I really fail to see how I can achieve this for you," I protested. " Do you take me to be some kind of magician ? "

" You are being singularly obtuse. What I wish you

to do is to find a new-born male child and bring it to a cottage near to the Hall where I shall go into confinement. The cottage belongs to the midwife who will be delivering my baby. If I am delivered of a healthy male child, then the child that you bring will be given to a village family to bring up. If my child transpires to be a girl, or a male child that appears unlikely to survive, we will make an exchange with a healthy child that you are providing."

I considered this for a minute or so. " It seems to me," I objected, that there will be some kind of difficulty here. I am not, after all, a trained baby nurse. I have no experience whatsoever in caring for new-born babies. I assume that I am to take the baby from some orphanage or other institution that deals in such matters. And such an institution should be some way away from where you are to give birth, otherwise tongues might start to wag."

" Yes ? "

" You wish me to be responsible for the safety of a new-born baby that I carry the length of England on a train ? How shall I feed it, to start with ? "

" This is why I am paying your employers a large sum of money. I am presenting you with a problem, and it is your task to solve this problem."

Once again I was lost in thought for one or two minutes. " Would it make much difference to your plans if I were to supply a baby of a few weeks old, rather than a few days old ? " I asked.

She pondered this. " I do not think so," she said. " There are few in the Hall who have experience of this kind of thing, and I do not think that a week or two will make very much difference in the perception of those around me."

" When is all this to be accomplished ? " I asked. " How long do I have to prepare this ? "

For answer, she looked down at her stomach. " I am between five and six months gone," she told me. " You will receive word through the messenger who dispatched you here when your services are required. I will supply you with details of the cottage and the woman who will receive the baby in a week or so."

It struck me that although there was no immediate need for action, when the time did come, it would be necessary for me to move fast, and to have everything in preparation ready for the event. I said this to her, and she appeared pleased. " You are obviously the right man for the job," she remarked approvingly.

" I hope that I can make plans which will come to fruition along with the best of them," I said, more than a little flattered by this appraisal.

She looked at me speculatively. " In the shorter scheme of things, what are your plans for this evening, John ? "

" I have nothing on hand."

" Excellent. In which case, let me order a bottle of champagne and a dozen of oysters for each of us, and we can enjoy a private evening together."

A few hours later I left her hotel room. " You know, I do not believe in the aphrodisiac properties of oysters any more," she said to me.

" What do you mean ? " I replied, a little chagrined. I believed that I had given sufficient satisfaction.

" You consumed the full dozen of your oysters, but only five of them had an effect," she answered with a straight face, but almost immediately burst out laughing. " Oh, John, you should have seen your own face just then. The vanity of men ! " She returned to seriousness. " I probably will not see you again until all this is completed, but I want you to know that I am delighted that it is you, and not some complete stranger, who is carrying out this errand for me." She threw her arms around my neck and kissed me. " Now go, John. Go, and do this for me, and I will be waiting for you when it is all over."

I walked back to my lodgings in a kind of daze. As I had said to Elizabeth, it would be necessary for me to make plans in advance so that when the day came all would be ready. I was under no illusions regarding her affection, though. I had more than sufficient knowledge of her behaviour in the past, and I had no reason to believe that it had in any way changed. Be that as it may, the memory of her soft skin and pliant limbs was pleasant, and carried me through the next few weeks as I laid my plans, making a journey up to Northumberland, and several to the West Country.

Some three months after my conversation with Elizabeth, I received word that the time was near and that I was to deliver a healthy male baby to Hareby Hall.

I began to make enquiries to start putting my plans in motion. By now I had access to many of the sources of information that fed Moriarty's network. My spies informed me that the gypsy encampment that I sought was presently somewhere outside Norwich, and I made my way there.

To my delight, my erstwhile companion, Mary, was still with the band, and professed herself delighted to be in my company once again. To my further satisfaction, she had recently given birth to a daughter, to whom she was still giving suck. This was an unexpected advantage to me in my plans. With the aid of a few sovereigns, I was able to persuade Mary's husband that she should accompany me, together with her baby, for a few days, and whatever I may have been to her in the past, this was now a matter of ancient history. I swore this to him by all that he and I held holy. I am of the opinion, though, that the golden coins I passed to him were stronger proof of my good faith than all the oaths that I swore.

Taking Mary with me, together with her babe, I travelled to Devon, where I had previously befriended the overseer of an orphanage in Taunton. You may smile to think of a smartly dressed gentlemen such as I travelling in company with a gypsy woman, but I was prepared for this, and while I was dressed as a respectable working man, Mary and her baby were clad in garments which I had supplied, matching my own apparent status. Naturally, we were not travelling first-class on the trains, and I am confident that we aroused no suspicion or curiosity in the minds of our fellow travellers.

Not trusting my own judgement in the matter of selecting babies—a procedure in which I had no experience whatsoever—I requested that Mary should select a fine healthy male baby not more than two weeks old. Happily, such an infant was available, and its little hand clung to Mary's finger as if it were that of its own mother. I paid the overseer the amount that we had previously agreed, and we departed Taunton. In the train compartment that we shared, with no other passengers to disturb our privacy, Mary fed both infants, and even

I, who do not consider myself in any way to being domestically inclined, was touched by the sight.

" What's going to happen to him, then ? " Mary asked me.

" It's all the toss of a coin," I told her. " If another woman has a girl, this little fellow will end up being a Lord's son. If she has a boy, he will grow up in a cottage."

" And if it's a girl, what's going to happen to that girl ? " Mary persisted.

" She'll be well looked after," I assured her. I had, indeed, made arrangements for another child to be cared for, no matter whether it was a boy or a girl of which Elizabeth was delivered.

" That's good to know." Mary seemed to be reassured by this news.

The train journey to the North was a long one, and we stopped at a hotel in the Midlands. True to the word that I had given to Mary's husband, we slept in separate beds. Indeed, I would have gone further and slept in a separate room, but Mary insisted that she had never slept alone in her life, and the prospect frightened her. Breakfast at the hotel was obviously an unfamiliar experience, but I was proud of her as she watched my movements and copied them. It occurred to me once more that were I to give up my present way of life, life with a group which included women such as Mary would be far from the worst choice I could make.

Eventually we reached Berwick-upon-Tweed, and I lodged Mary and her baby in an inn close to the station, taking the baby boy with me in a hired trap that I drove alone to the cottage where I was to deliver him. The door was opened to me by an old woman, whom I confirmed was the midwife who would be present at the confinement of Lady Elizabeth. She exclaimed over the infant, and I handed him over, together with some money. I had previously made arrangements with her for a certain sum of money, but she demanded guineas rather than pounds, and I was in little position to refuse her demands.

I was more than a little sad to leave the baby with her, having become slightly attached to it during the journey from Taunton, much to my surprise, as I had never fancied that I was susceptible to that kind of sentiment. I drove the trap back to Berwick, and met Mary at the hotel.

" Is he safe ? " she asked me anxiously. Obviously she too had taken a fancy to the little boy.

" I think so," I said to her. On reflection, I now know that I would never have left the baby in the care of the old woman had I not instinctively trusted her to care for him. If I have felt that he was in any way in danger of being maltreated or neglected, I am convinced that I would never have left him there. How I would have accomplished my mission, though, I do not know. Maybe I would simply have gone back to the gypsies with Mary and started a new life as a traveller.

In any event, my job as I saw it now was to return Mary and her baby back to her husband. Again we travelled as man and wife, passing the night in Lincoln as we had the previous night, in separate beds. I felt some sense of loss when I parted from Mary at her encampment, but I was happy to see her back in the life where she belonged among her own folk.

When I returned to London, I sent a message

reporting my actions, and a few days later received another visit, again unannounced, from Colonel Moran.

" We have received word from Hareby Hall," he began. " Lady Elizabeth was delivered of a girl a few days ago, and the substitution of the boy that you took up there was successfully accomplished. As far as the family is concerned, she was delivered of a boy."

I could not contain my curiosity. " What happened to her baby girl ? " I asked.

" I had heard that you had made arrangements for the unwanted child to be lodged with the family in the neighbourhood, but it appears that these were not needed. Lady Elizabeth found it impossible to part completely with her child, and has secreted it, with a wet nurse, in a hidden chamber in a remote part of the Hall. Naturally," he added, anticipating my next question, " I have no idea of its eventual fate."

" I take it we may regard this operation as having been a success, then ? "

" Yes. We are very pleased with the work you have done. The professor asked me to congratulate you, and to let you know that there will be a bonus payment made to you for the efficient way in which carried out the work." He dug in his coat pocket and withdrew a small leather pouch which he extended to me. I took it in my hand, feeling the weight of the many sovereigns that it contained.

" I do not wish it," I protested, returning the bag to him. " I would prefer to regard this as having been a favour performed for a friend, rather than work performed for hire."

Moran lifted his eyebrows. " A strange point of view," he commented. " Most in our organisation would be grateful for the professor's offer and generosity." Though no threat was explicitly stated, there was a certain menace in his voice which led me to believe that there might be adverse consequences should I fail to accept the money which was being offered to me.

" Very good, I will accept the professor's generosity. Please convey my gratitude to him." I took the bag in my hand, once again feeling the comforting weight of the coins within.

" Good man," he smiled, rising and resting his hand heavily on my shoulder. " Remember, we always expect you to agree with the professor. You do understand this, being an intelligent man, I am sure." His hand gripped my shoulder painfully. " By the by, we have a new crop of cheques for your attention. Please try to be a little more careful with the liquid in the future." His finger flicked the white spot on my forehead where I had touched the brush to it some months before. He bade me farewell, and left.

You may be wondering why I was hesitant to take the money. You may also wonder why I took the money at the last. As to the first, my answer was at least partly true. Though I was one of many to Lady Elizabeth, and I had no illusions regarding this, I was vain enough to believe that there was still some kind of special relationship between us. What I had done was, to some extent at any rate, performed as an act of friendship. There was also some kind of morality at work within me, a revulsion against trafficking in children, which this seemed to be. But as Moran talked to me, threatening me with the professor, it occurred to me that the money could be put to good use. I had a plan in mind.

About two weeks later I was told that Sherlock

The History of John Augustus Edward Clay As Told by Himself

Holmes had visited Hareby Hall in Northumberland, some weeks earlier and he, or his companion Dr Watson, had been responsible for saving the life of Elizabeth's husband. I had no definite information as to whether Elizabeth had in any way been involved in the incident, but knowing her as I did, I had a very strong suspicion that that she had had a hand in this.

It struck me that it would be of some advantage for me to learn more about this Sherlock Holmes, and I spent a little time outside his rooms in Baker Street, and one day followed a man whom I believed at the time to be Holmes himself, but I later discovered to be John Watson, into Hyde Park. I fear I must have been rather careless in my scrutiny of the man, for he noticed my observation of him, and started away.* I was, however, unable to catch a glimpse of Sherlock Holmes in person, despite my best efforts in that direction. Indeed, my first face-to-face encounter with Holmes, whom I did not recognise at the time, was immediately prior to my arrest following the little game of the Red-Headed League.

I was anxious to see Lady Elizabeth on her return to London from Northumberland, but this was not to be the case. I, along with all other readers of the London newspapers, was horrified to learn of her death on the railway in the suburbs of London, following the tragic death by drowning of her husband at the Hall and the unmasking of a scandal involving the substitution of a new-born infant. I could not believe for a minute that her death had been an accident, but a veil of silence

---

* Dr. Watson confirms this sighting in his account of the incident in *The Darlington Substitution*.

appeared to have been drawn around the incident, and I could discover almost nothing about the circumstances.

I made discreet enquiries about the infants at Hareby, and discovered that the substitution had been uncovered by no less a personage than Sherlock Holmes. The little girl, Elizabeth's natural child, had been taken into the family, and was apparently loved and cared for. As for the baby boy, for whom I continued to feel some affection, I was pleased to learn that he was being brought up within the household as a companion to his foster-sister, and would lack for nothing in his life. Even though the operation may be regarded overall as a failure, in that Elizabeth Hareby failed to inherit the Darlington estate, the blame for the failure was not laid at my door, and I continued to enjoy the high regard of Professor Moriarty and his henchmen.

John Clay speaks 5: The orphanage

HAVE READ JOHN WATSON'S ACCOUNT of the Red-Headed League, and there is one part in it of which I am particularly proud. It is the point where Inspector Jones tells his audience that he never knows where I will be at any one time.

He says to them, " He'll crack a crib in Scotland one week, and be raising money to build an orphanage in Cornwall the next". His implication, though, is that my activities with regard to the orphanage were fraudulent—that I was collecting money under false pretences. Nothing, I wish to state most clearly, could be further from the truth.

I mentioned that I was rather taken with the baby I took to Hareby Hall. I had never considered a future as a family man, but there was something in that small pink crumpled face that touched something inside me. I've never been one of those who feel it necessary to hide all their softer feelings, in case they should be thought of as being less than " real men". Colonel Moran was one whom I would put in that category. Almost never did I see him exhibit traces of humanity, or the gentler emotions. And yet, I flatter myself that I am no less a man than he. Many ladies of my acquaintance have been able to verify this from their personal experience. Whatever the reasons that men like Moran may have for their bluster and swagger, they are not mine.

While I am on the subject of Jones, I would like to add a few words to the comments made by him at that time. He made the extraordinary claim that, " I've been on his track for years, and have never set eyes on him yet". This was simply an absurd statement on the part of the police agent. For once I am in full agreement with Sherlock Holmes, who told Watson, who repeated this opinion in writing, that he believed Jones to be an " absolute imbecile". There is no way that Inspector Jones, had he wished to see me, or even to speak with me, could have found any reason not to do so. I lived in London under my own name, and I was tolerably well known in Society. Jones would merely have had to ring the bell on my front door to be admitted to my presence. However, had he wished to take me into custody or to charge me with offences, he would have found this to be a much more onerous proposition.

Among the other benefits of working for Moriarty's organisation, we enjoyed the services of some of the country's top legal experts in criminal defence. Any attempt to bring charges, or even to bring me to the station for questioning, would have met with spirited opposition, and possible counter-charges for wrongful arrest and detention and so on. I doubt Jones was fully aware of this, but if he had attempted such a move, all this would have been brought to his attention very rapidly. On the other hand, Sherlock Holmes, from everything I could gather from Moran and others, was well aware of the extent and the powers of the organisation for which I was working. In addition, being a private agent and not one of the official police, he had to take great care not to overstep the bounds set by the law. You will remember that my arrest came as the result of being caught red-handed, even though Holmes had made a series of deductions which might have been considered to constitute sufficient grounds for arrest had he been a member of the Metropolitan police force.

As I say, I was moved by the baby, and sometimes even considered going to Hareby to look in on him, but dismissed the idea, simply on the grounds that it would draw undue attention. I did, however, consider the orphanage from which I had brought the infant. Though it was clean, and the children appeared to be adequately cared for, the overseer had told me that it was incapable of taking in all the children presented to it. The reason as it was explained to me was that there was an insufficient number of such institutions in that part of the country, and as a result, the one from which I took the baby was overflowing.

I made some enquiries as to how much it would cost to set up and endow an orphanage capable of meeting the needs of some twenty children, and was surprised how little money was actually needed. I had supposed that such an enterprise could only be carried out by a wealthy landowner or industrialist, but it turned out that I actually had half the necessary money saved away already. As I mentioned, I lived well within my means, and my everyday needs were being met by Moriarty.

I accordingly set my goal—to found such an orphanage in Cornwall, where I had been informed there was a particular shortage of such institutions, and to ensure that it continued to receive money for its support, even without my help.

I knew it was useless to ask Moriarty to contribute towards this aim, but I had devised a way which would allow me to start my work without further delay. I therefore sent a message via the usual route, asking for a meeting with the head of the organisation. I was almost certain that my request would be granted, and was thus unsurprised when a carriage drew up outside my residence, and the driver announced that he was to take me to " meet the Chief", as he put it.

" You don't mind, guv, if we pull the blinds, do you ? " he said, suiting the action to his words. This had never occurred before, and it came to me that I was possibly being taken to Moriarty's actual residence, the location of which was known to very few in the organisation.

Though I have a good knowledge of the streets of London, possibly as good as that of Mr. Holmes as described by Dr. Watson, I could not tell where we were, other than that we had crossed the river at some point and were now on the Surrey side. After some thirty-five minutes by my watch, the carriage stopped, and the driver opened the door. " Straight in, if you would, sir," he said. It was more in the nature of an order than a request, and I stepped out of the carriage almost straight into the hallway of what appeared to be a comfortable suburban villa.

" This way, sir," said a bowing butler, ushering me into a well-appointed drawing-room, where Professor Moriarty was seated in an armchair.

" Pray be seated," he invited, waving me to a chair opposite him. " What can I do for you ? " he began, without any preliminary conversation.

" This may seem like a strange request, but I would like to receive one half of the proceeds from the next large operation."

As I had anticipated, this demand had his full attention. He sat up straight in his chair, and regarded me with his strange unblinking eyes. " For the next operation alone ? " he asked, a touch of incredulity in his voice.

" Yes, and I would like to pay it back out of the earnings of subsequent tasks," I added. " You would not pay me my usual share until that balanced the larger amount. With interest, if you like," I added.

" In other words, you want an advance ? " asked Moriarty. " My dear Clay, that can easily be arranged, on one condition."

" That being ? " I asked, though I already believed I knew the answer.

" That I know why you need the money. I do not believe the answer is horses or cards in your case. Women, maybe ? " There was no hint of salaciousness in this comment, which was offered in an offhand, almost dispassionate tone.

I shook my head. " I am afraid I would prefer not to tell you. It may sound rather ridiculous."

He shook his head. " In that case, I cannot accede to your request. If I am to loan money, I wish to know the purpose."

" Believe me, sir," I said to him, " this is not for any purpose that works against your aims, or your operations. My only reason for not informing you of the purpose of this is my fear that you will find it ridiculous, and laugh at me."

Naturally, as I had intended, this hooked him still further. " I cannot promise that I will not laugh at you," he answered me at last, " but I will listen to what you have to say and endeavour to take it seriously."

" Very well, then. I wish to build an orphanage. To start such an institution, and ensure that it has sufficient funds to continue."

Moriarty sat back in surprise, and stared at me in silence for a good two minutes. At last, he spoke. " I cannot begin to understand you, Clay. You are one of my most trusted lieutenants, and with good reason. You do your work well and efficiently. You have taken on assignments that I had believed were almost impossible to perform, and carried them out to perfection. And yet... " He paused. " Yet you have this aversion to the use of violence in your work, or indeed, any work in which you are involved. And now this ! " He fell silent once more, and continued to regard me with that strange reptilian gaze. I held my peace, feeling that an interruption would in no way serve my purpose.

" If you were not so infernally good at what you do, I do not see that I could keep you working for me," he said, after two or three of the most uncomfortable minutes that I have ever spent in my life. There was no anger in his voice, but there was a coldness of manner that frightened me in the same way as his threats had done at the time of our first meeting. " Very well, then," he replied in that same flat tone. " I will give instructions to allow you to carry out your wishes. As it happens, the next job that I have for you is indeed an important one. I have received word that a large valuable consignment of gemstones is on its way from South Africa. In order to frustrate the workings of persons in our line of business," and here he smiled mirthlessly, " the stones will enter this country through the Port of Glasgow. Once they have reached this country, they will be stored in a location where the owner of the diamonds believes them to be safe. However, as both you and I are well aware, there is no such thing as a safe location. I wish you to lead a small party to recover those stones for me. On successful completion of the task, you will receive one half of the proceeds. This will, I assure you, be a considerable sum. Colonel Moran will supply you with the full details at the appropriate time, including the names of your party, as well as any relevant information regarding the diamonds and the location in which they are to be stored. I trust this is satisfactory to you ? "

There was, of course, no question of its being anything other than satisfactory to me. Indeed, I was well pleased to get away from London for a while. For some time Colonel Moran had been warning me about the activities of Sherlock Holmes, who seemed to be following my moves with alarming accuracy, but he was not close enough to be able to prove my involvement in any of the cases which he was investigating.

The gang that I led up to Glasgow was a group of skilled workmen, who were able to turn their hand to many different types of labour. One or two of them could quite easily pass as tradesmen or as clerks as well as workers, and all were quick-witted and, what was important to me, were prepared to follow my orders.

I do not propose to go into great detail here as to how we cracked the Glasgow crib and retrieved the diamonds for Moriarty. I was proud of the fact that my men obeyed my wishes, and no violence was used in the achievement of this goal. Indeed, the only injuries sustained during the whole operation were two broken fingers. These belonged to our leading cracksman, and were broken in the course of opening the safe door. Naturally, his medical needs were taken care of.

I returned to London, to discover Colonel Moran on my doorstep. " Congratulations on a job well done," he remarked gruffly. " I have been talking to the professor about your lunatic scheme, and he has decided that you may spend the next six weeks putting it into practice."

" And the money ? " I asked him.

For answer, he tossed over a bag of significantly more than the usual size. I caught it, and almost staggered under its weight as he grinned at me. " The Glasgow stones fetched a good price in Amsterdam, you'll be pleased to know. That's half of it that you have in your hands. Happy now ? I tell you, though, it will take you some time to pay things back like this. Oh, and by the way, I advise you to leave London as soon as possible. That Sherlock Holmes still seems to be on your trail."

" About the Glasgow job ? "

" No. As far as I know, no one has any idea who is behind that. You're safe on that account, at least. This is all about one of the IOUs that you produced for use in the Nonpareil Club. Somehow it seems that your name has got attached to it."

" Then there is a traitor in the ranks ! " I exclaimed. Indeed, I was pretty much convinced of this, and I had my suspicions as to the identity of the traitor. " I had no connection other than to supply the IOU."

" We are looking into it," he assured me. " In any case, I advise you to make your way to Cornwall as soon as possible."

With that he left me, with my mind ill at ease. There was little doubt, I felt, that it was Colonel Moran and no other who was supplying information to Sherlock Holmes or the authorities, but probably to the former, out of jealousy for my current success and high standing with Professor Moriarty. Naturally, I had no proof of any of this, and I was unwilling to confront Moran directly with my accusation. Of course, I considered the possibility that Moran was being less than truthful when he informed me that Sherlock Holmes was on my trail. It is quite possible that he wished to use those six weeks in which I would be in Cornwall to consolidate his position within Moriarty's organisation.

In any case, I was anxious to get my orphanage started. More importantly, I wish to recruit support for the project from among the local people, so that it would continue long after the original money was exhausted.

I opened the bag that had been so casually tossed to me, and was amazed at the amount of money it contained. I knew that we had done a good job in Glasgow, but I had no idea of how efficient Moriarty's methods

THE HISTORY OF JOHN AUGUSTUS EDWARD CLAY AS TOLD BY HIMSELF

of disposing of the loot that we had acquired had been. I calculated that the money that I held in my hands, when added to my savings, was more than enough to start the orphanage that I had in mind.

I made my way to Cornwall, to the little town of Looe, where I planned to set up the orphanage. It was intoxicating to discover the power of money, which I was spending freely, almost for the first time in my life. Powered by the lure of the sovereigns that I was bestowing, workmen were building and hammering and sawing at a rate which was far in excess of their usual speed.

In the meantime, I was engaging the services of the local vicar, the Reverend Roundhay*, to act as the chairman of the Board that would oversee the orphanage. I presented myself as a businessman from London who had come into unexpected wealth as the result of investments on the Stock Exchange, and who wished to use the money for the betterment of others. The good man accepted my story without question, and readily agreed to serve in the capacity I proposed for him.

" I have little enough to do here, if truth be told," he said to me. " I have an interest in the archaeology of this region, and it keeps me active, but it can hardly be considered as ' good works', in my opinion. Your charity will not only be the saving of many children from destitution and poverty, but will also rescue a middle-aged

---

* Note in Dr. Watson's handwriting. " Holmes and I came into contact with the very same reverend gentleman following his removal from Looe to the village of Tredannick Wollas in the same county. Naturally, neither of us had any idea that he had been in contact with John Clay earlier. I have described the events that took place during our stay in Cornwall elsewhere as *The Adventure of the Devil's Foot*."

clergyman from the sin of sloth." He beamed at me. Little did he know that the money which supported the worthy aim that he was supporting had been gained by unlawful means, and that he was presently in conversation with the agent who had gained it in that way.

My next task was to ensure that the orphanage could continue its work, and the Reverend Roundhay and I toured the houses of the local gentry, such as they were, exacting promises from them that they would continue to support the orphanage in the future. The mere title of Patron was often enough to open their purse-strings, and with Roundhay's continued presence in the area, I was sure that the money would continue flowing. Indeed, we worked well as a team, and I was filled with admiration for the way in which he was able to wheedle and cajole these people into supporting our aims. He, for his part, was complimentary about my part in this.

" Upon my life, sir," he said to me as we were returning in the dogcart following a particularly successful visit to a local squire. " As our Irish friends would say, you have the gift of the blarney about you, and you are doing the work of the Lord. My word, sir, you would make a capital preacher were you to throw up your business and take Holy Orders."

I smiled inwardly, thinking that this is exactly what my father had intended for me as a career. With my past career, though, I felt it was extremely unlikely that I would be accepted as a candidate for ordination. I confess, though, that on seeing the life of my new friend, I could think of worse futures for myself than this.

Eventually, the orphanage was finished, and I felt that I had left its organisation and upkeep in capable hands. I left Looe, but vowed to return regularly to see the results of my efforts, and I kept my promise, visiting several times each year.

Of all the actions I have undertaken in my life, this is the one of which I am most proud. Though Moran and Moriarty were both aware of my action, it to was hardly ever mentioned by them again—indeed, Moran never mentioned it at all—and I was left to contemplate my accomplishment alone. I am only writing this now, indeed, as I do not want posterity to think of me merely in the terms in which Dr. Watson described me.*

JOHN CLAY SPEAKS 6: THE SMASHER

N MY RETURN from Looe to London, I discovered that my earlier premonitions were well founded. Colonel Moran seemed to have further secured his place in Moriarty's organisation, together with that of several of his immediate friends and cronies, at my expense.

The tasks on which I was now employed seemed to be of less importance than previously, and while Moran

---

* Note in Dr. Watson's handwriting. " This whole episode as described by Clay sounds too fantastic to be true. Why would a man who, by his own confession, was a hardened criminal, take his ill-gotten gains to perform such an act of charity ? Nonetheless, I made enquiries, and discovered that this account given here was substantially correct. Truly a sign that every human soul is composed of more threads, both black and white, than we care to admit to ourselves."

had previously given me instructions in person when we needed to take face-to-face, such orders were now conveyed by underlings. There was nothing explicitly stated by anyone, but I had the impression that my services were either not as valued as they had been in the past, or at least that the results of my efforts were not being presented in a way that did me justice.

One of these messengers from the Colonel was a man of about my age, or a little older, named Archibald Stamford*. From the first time I met him, I liked his friendly face, topped with a shock of bright red hair. After a few meetings, he appeared to drop his guard enough to confide in me that he was less than content with the way in which Colonel Moran was handling matters. However, despite my liking for the man, I suspected him of being one of Moran's *agents provocateurs*, attempting to make me utter some words against the Colonel which could later be used as proof of my disloyalty. I held my peace, and continued to obey the instructions I was given. I did my work well, and it was a matter of only a few months before I had repaid the debt I owed in the matter of the orphanage.

Stamford and I continued our acquaintanceship, and we started working together on a number of jobs. After a short while, I was persuaded that his feelings towards the Colonel were indeed as he described them, and that he was indeed less than contented with the way

---

* Editor's note: This is obviously the same " Archie Stamford" as described as being " taken" near Farnham (*The Solitary Cyclist*). However, this must have occurred early in Holmes' career, and his sentence must have been a relatively light one, as stated here, otherwise it is hard to reconcile Clay's narrative with Watson's.

in which affairs were being managed. He, along with me, felt that his experience and skills entitled him to better treatment.

He had previously served a prison sentence for forgery, having been convicted of uttering false cheques, and his Nemesis on this occasion had been the mysterious Sherlock Holmes, whose name now seemed to be appearing at every turn.

" Tall cove, he is, with a pair of eyes in his head that you wouldn't believe unless you saw them and a nose that sticks out in front of him. Those eyes miss nothing about you when he looks you up and down. He seems like a skinny kind of beggar," said Archie of the detective, " but my eye, he's strong enough when he lays hold of you. He's got a friend with him, a sawbones, who writes down everything he says and does. Wants to make a blooming hero of him.*"

I have subsequently encountered Sherlock Holmes, albeit briefly, and I have to say that Archie (for we soon found ourselves on Christian name terms) had rather exaggerated the prominence of his nose. I have also met and talked with Dr. John Watson on more than one occasion, and found him to be a pleasant enough gentleman, with more interest in setting down the exact truth and possessing a greater sense of fairness than Archie gave him credit for. Still, Archie's account was necessarily somewhat biased, given that the result of his encounter was a few years as a guest of Her Majesty, God bless her.

---

* Note in Watson's handwriting: " I was amused by this description of Sherlock Holmes and myself, and showed it to my friend, without mentioning the source. He laughed heartily at the portrait painted here of him and me."

As a forger, Archie's skills left something to be desired, in my opinion. He lacked the education and imagination that are needed to think oneself into the character of the man whose writing is being copied. Sheer mechanical duplication is not enough in these cases. It is necessary to think oneself into the part. I have heard that the same is true of those who make their living producing facsimiles of works of art. It is not enough to paint like the artist whose work is being replicated—one must almost become that artist in order to produce the painting.

Be that as it may, Archie and I were the top of the tree as regards forgery in Moriarty's little organisation, or so we believed. It was a shock to us when we were informed that our next job was to go to the Midlands and dispose of some forged banknotes that had been acquired from a Belgian source.

" I'm not a bleeding smasher,*" complained Archie, but he knew as well as I did that we had little or no choice in the matter. Accordingly, we took ourselves to Birmingham with the pile of paper, and proceeded to distribute it among the various banks in the region.

" It's not even as if it's good soft," Archie said to me, as we were sitting enjoying a quiet evening in the saloon bar of a public house in Five Ways. " I reckon I could do a better job than I could with my eyes closed, and I know you could for sure, John."

I didn't answer, but considered something I had heard just before we had left London.

" Archie, do you want to get back into the Chief's

---

* Editor's note: " Smasher" was a 19th century underworld term for a passer of forged currency.

good books ? " I asked him. Archie always referred to Moriarty as " the Chief".

" You know that I do. That b____ Moran is keeping me back. You too, John."

" Well, I know that this isn't the sort of thing that you usually do, but I heard something that would put us both back in favour with the Chief if we were able to pull it off. We'd have to keep Moran out of the picture, so he couldn't cut in on us and steal all the credit."

" What are you talking about ? "

I informed him of what I had overheard in the City. I had heard, while waiting for an acquaintance in a club, that a branch of a bank in Aldersgate Street, the City and Suburban, was expecting to strengthen its reserves, and was preparing to borrow a stock of gold coins from France. I could tell that Archie had little understanding of the financial machinations that would lead to such an event, but the mention of gold coins caught his interest.

" How much do you think it's going to be ? "

" I heard it was going to be about a hundred thousand pounds*," I told him.

Archie sat back, suitably impressed and took a pull at his beer. " That's worth going for," he agreed. " Will you use the same mob that you used in Glasgow ? "

I told him that the two of us were going to do the job on our own, and he looked at me in some astonishment.

" You're off your rocker, mate," he said to me. " How can we blag that much, just the two of us ? "

---

* Editor's note: Clay had been misinformed, or was deliberately misleading his confederate. We know that the bank's Mr. Merryweather informed Sherlock Holmes that the loan was of 20,000 napoleons and Holmes calculated this as being equal to £30,000.

" I have an idea how we can pull it off. And you know another thing ? The Chief is sending Moran over to Switzerland for a month or so. He needn't know anything about it. With him away, I think I can talk the Chief into letting us go for it."

" If you pull this off, John, with just the two of us involved, you're a b_____ genius, I tell you."

We disposed of the rest of the banknotes in the next few days, and I can tell you, I was heartily glad to be rid of them. I never did discover how much the Belgian was paid for them, but whatever the amount, it was too high in my opinion. Every time I passed one over the counter, I was expecting to be nibbed, as Archie would have put it.

We went back to London with our bags full of real cash, and, as I had predicted to Archie, Moran was absent from the city, which made it more pleasant in my opinion. When the cash was being transferred, I asked the messenger to take a message to Moriarty, asking for an interview.

The request was granted, and the same method of transporting me to his house as previously was employed. A carriage drew up, and it took me, with the blinds drawn as before, across the river to an unknown destination.

Moriarty lounged in the chair where I had seen him on the previous occasion. He seemed not to have moved in the months since we last spoke, and he regarded me with a quizzical air.

" What is it this time, Clay ? You wish to found a monastery, or perhaps this time it is a mission to save the souls of fallen women ? " He smiled, to indicate that he was joking. " To return to seriousness, have you had word how your little enterprise in the West Country is coming along ? "

As it happened, I had received a report the previous morning, delivered to my post office box, in which the orphanage was described as flourishing, with some twenty infants being provided for. The statement accompanying the report showed that the financial health of the institution rivalled that of the infants for which it was caring. I explained this to Moriarty, who appeared to be listening with great interest.

" Well done," he said at last. " You seem to show an impressive talent for organisation and attention to detail. I have a good mind to promote you to take the place of Colonel Moran as my chief of operations."

I protested against this. Such a move would almost certainly set the Colonel against me still further and result in a rivalry in which I was almost sure I would end up as the loser. " Before I could consider taking such a position—and believe me, I am sensible of the honour here—I have an opportunity which I think may be of interest." I told Moriarty about the City and Suburban Bank's loan of the gold, and that I believed Archie Stamford and I could take it.

" I had heard of this, too, but had no idea how to obtain the gold. What is your plan, Clay ? "

" I have no plan as yet, sir," I told him. " Give me three days, and I will have a plan, though. I am confident that Stamford and I can take this alone, without violence and without bloodshed. Since only two of us will be involved, I will ensure that the expenses are kept to a minimum. It may take some three or four months, but I promise you we can do it."

" From any man other than you, I would regard this

as an outrageous boast," he said. " You have three months, no more, to carry out your plan. And two days, not three, to inform me of it. At the end of that time, send me your proposal in writing. The usual cypher." He turned away, and I knew I was dismissed.

The next two days saw me engaged in walking up and down Aldersgate-street, examining the bank, as well as those streets and thoroughfares surrounding it. I even entered the bank, posing as a potential customer, and was shown into the manager's office. On my way there, I noted a set of stairs leading down to a cellar, which I could guess was used as a vault. The doors and other barriers within the bank appeared to be of a strength and thickness that would prevent Archie and me from breaking through. But the cellar could prove to be an Achilles' heel, I guessed.

If, I reasoned, the buildings behind the bank or next to it were also provided with a cellar, and if it were possible to gain access to that cellar on a regular basis, I guessed that Archie and I could dig our way to the gold. On one side of the bank was a restaurant of some kind. I could guess that the basement of that would be used as a kitchen, and this was confirmed by the odours arising from the grating at my feet. The other side was a small newspaper shop, owned by a squint-eyed man seemingly of uncertain sobriety, which did not appear to be in the least promising.

I left the main thoroughfare and entered a small mean-looking square, Saxe-Coburg-square, containing a number of shops, one of which, a pawnbroker's on the corner, appeared to be directly behind the bank. I went up to the shop and read the notice in the window.

" Assistant required. Apply within." I rang the bell,

The History of John Augustus Edward Clay As Told by Himself

as the shop door appeared to be locked, and a young servant-girl answered.

" I've come about the job," I told her. " Is Mr. Wilson in ? " The owner's name, Jabez Wilson, was prominently displayed beside the three balls above the door.

" He's out. Have you come about the advertisement ? " she asked me.

" No, I just saw the card on the door."

" Himself won't see you if you haven't replied to the advertisement in the newspaper. In writing," she told me.

" Which newspaper ? "

" I don't know. The usual ones, I suppose. Whatever they are. You think I've got time to sit around reading them ? "

" Very good," I said, and returned to the drunken newsagent's, where in consideration of a small sum, I was permitted to buy all the papers for the last week that might conceivably carry the advertisement.

I took them back to my home, and soon found what I was looking for.

Giving my name as " Vincent Spaulding", the name of a loathed and feared House Captain from my days at Eton, I wrote a letter in a none-too-literate hand to Jabez Wilson, offering to work for low wages, as I wished to learn the pawnbroking trade.

He answered my missive by return of post, inviting me to Saxe-Coburg-square, and the first thing that I noticed about him was his hair, which was as fiery red as that of my colleague Archie. Surely, I felt, as I sat through his endless prattle as to how I was to conduct myself in my time with him, there was a way to make use of this coincidence. In a flash it came to me, and as soon I could make my escape, I made my way back home, refining the details of my plan as I did so. By the time I reached my abode, I had it all worked out in every detail, and I set down my thoughts, and sent them to Moriarty.

John Clay speaks 7: The Red-Headed League

On receiving permission from Moriarty to carry out my scheme, I told Archie that we were ready to start work.

" What's your plan, then ? " he asked me.

" I've got a new crib," I told him. " It's a pawnbroker's just behind the bank, and they have a cellar there. We can get into the bank vaults from there, I am sure. We can dig our way in."

" But if you're meant to be working there ? "

" I'm taking up photography," I told him. Archie looked puzzled.

" What for ? " he asked in bewilderment.

" Because," I explained to him, " it needs a dark place to develop the pictures. And can you think of a darker place than a cellar ? "

For the first week, I submitted to Wilson's tuition on the duties of a pawnbroker's assistant. As you might imagine, these are not exactly onerous, but the old fool kept on giving me the same instructions several times.

Despite my newly acquired hobby of photography, I saw that there was no possibility of my ever breaking through to the bank in the time that Moriarty had allowed me. It was obvious that both Archie and I would have to work on the project together, and work hard—harder than was possible with Wilson always calling me from upstairs. It was clear that we would have to keep him away for at least a part of the day to allow us time for our excavations. The girl who did the cooking and some housework could be discounted—she seemed to be possessed of little curiosity in the affairs of others. Indeed, I sometimes suspected her of being more than a little simple.

The mornings and early afternoons seemed to me to be the most suitable times that Mr. Jabez Wilson should be elsewhere. For some reason, a pawnbroker's customers seem to prefer the evenings, especially towards the end of a week, to do their business. Perhaps they feel that they won't be seen by their neighbours ? In any event, Wilson liked to mind the business in person at those times, reserving Tuesday night alone for the meetings of the Freemasons' Lodge that he attended on those nights of the week.

I pondered hard on what stratagem would be most effective in removing him from the shop at other times, and was ruminating on the strange coincidence of he and Archie both possessing singularly striking and distinctive heads of red hair, when my stroke of genius (and I do not believe that I am being unduly modest when I describe it in those terms) came to me.

The next day, I showed Archie an advertisement in the newspaper.

" TO THE RED-HEADED LEAGUE—On account of the

bequest of the late Ezikiah Hopkins, of Lebanon, Penn., U.S.A., there is now another vacancy open which entitles a member of the League to a salary of four pounds a week for purely nominal services. All red-headed men who are sound in body and mind, and above the ages of twenty-one years, are eligible. Apply in person on Monday, at eleven o'clock, to Duncan Ross, at the offices of the League, 7 Pope's Court, Fleet-street."

" That sounds like a berth worth shipping for," said Archie. " Think I'd stand a chance ? "

" No, you juggins," I told him. " You are Duncan Ross."

He scratched his head. " Why ? "

I was about to curse him as a thick-headed fool, when I remembered that he had never clapped eyes on Wilson. " Because, my dear Archie," I told him, " both you and Mr. Jabez Wilson, my employer of the moment, have this wonderful thing in common about you. You both have red hair."

I must give Archie some credit. It took him a very short space of time to work out what I had in mind. " That's capital ! " he cried. " How will we make him fill his time all day ? "

" We'll just keep him at it for four hours a day. I don't want him to chuck it halfway through because he gets bored. I know," I said. " We'll get him to copy out the Encyclopedia Britannica—see how far he gets with the letter ' A' in the next few months. I'll make sure that he sees the advertisement, and I'll bring him to you in Pope's Court, where I have arranged for the office, and you take him on at four pounds a week."

" Oh, you're a joker, you are, John ! But you must

coach me in my part. Tell me what I have to say and do when you bring him to me."

" Indeed so. We must also trick you out for the occasion. We wish Mr. Jabez Wilson to meet a worthy representative of the late Ezikiah Hopkins, do we not ? "

I have to confess that Archie made a convincing representative of the Red-Headed League, and when he met Wilson at the room I had rented, he played his part to perfection, even seizing the pawnbroker's hair and pulling it hard—an action which I felt fully repaid the nagging I had experienced at his hands. I have read Dr. Watson's account of Wilson's relation of the events at Pope's Court, and I do not think I could better it. There is one small point which might be of interest. I thought it would be amusing if Wilson had to expend some of his own money to gain the sovereigns I was to pay him each week, and we acoordingly made it a condition of his "employment" that he should provide his own pen and paper.

So, with the bumbling old fool tucked safely away and working his way through the alphabet, as Dr. Watson has described him doing, Archie and I went to work. We were in luck, as the cellar floor was loose and allowed us to start our excavations with some ease. The tunnelling was not in the least easy, though, and we were at a loss as to where to store the earth that we removed, until we stumbled into a mysterious disused underground chamber with a single door that seemed to lead to a dead end blocked by soil, presumably once the cellar of a previous structure that had stood on the site. We used this chamber as a repository for the debris from our tunnel.

We had setbacks. At one point the tunnel collapsed, and I was forced to dig Archie out from a pile of loose earth and rubble, which would have stifled him had he remained buried in it. It was nearly eight weeks before the tunnel was completed to our satisfaction, and it was a red-letter day when I poked my shovel upwards to discover the flagstones that made up the floor of the bank's vault.

I should mention that almost at the end of the course of our excavations, indeed, just after we had reached the bank vault, I was visited by Sherlock Holmes and Dr. Watson. Although I had seen Dr. Watson previously, as I mentioned earlier in my account of the Darlington substitution, I failed to recognise him on this occasion. Indeed, I paid little attention to these visitors, who merely wished to know the way to the Strand, and I gave them the first answer that came into my head. As I closed the door on the visitors, though, I remembered that the one who had asked the question of me had failed to meet my eye, but had instead kept his gaze directed downward. After he was out of sight, I glanced down, and noted that the knees of my trousers were in a noticeably less than pristine condition, but failed to attach much importance to this.

Anyway, as I mentioned, we had arrived at what I took to be the bank vault, and I carefully lifted one stone and shone a lantern around the room thus revealed. It was certainly a vault, and the crates that I beheld, clearly marked with the stamp of the Banque de France, almost certainly contained the gold of which I had heard.

" We're there, Archie ! " I told him. " We'll do the job at the weekend, and they won't notice a thing until the Monday, by which time Vincent Spaulding will have ceased to be."

" And the Red-Headed League ? "

" I suppose we'd better close it down. You can do that, Archie. Just post a notice on the door saying that the League has closed down or something along those lines."

What I did not know was that Archie was fool enough to go away and do what I had suggested almost as soon as I had told him to do it. This sudden loss of the weekly four sovereigns had obviously annoyed Wilson, who had gone off in a huff to see Sherlock Holmes, and it was that which had prompted the visit by him to my door. If he'd only waited another day or so...

Still, there's no point in crying over the milk that was spilled. Archie was one of the best, but it was my fault to trust him with a piece of business like that. I will say, though, that he was smart enough to leave a false trail for Wilson to follow when he closed the lease on the office we had rented. He picked an address at random, and I was amused to read later in Watson's account that Wilson had actually gone there and discovered it to be a manufactory of artificial knee-caps.

We prepared ourselves for the removal of the gold, which was planned for a Saturday night. Dark lanterns we had already, of course. We prepared slings and ropes for the removal of the crates from the vault into the tunnel, and a small wheeled trolley to move them back into the empty cellar where we had deposited the earth. From there, we would move them out to a waiting wagon on the Sunday night.

I am afraid that Archie and I were guilty of the sin of counting our chickens before they were hatched. We were already determining at which restaurant we would celebrate, and anticipating the fall from grace of Colonel Moran as we crept along the tunnel to the vault.

I will say this much for Sherlock Holmes; that he had everything well organised. It was the work of a minute for both Archie and me to be nabbed. You can probably imagine the shock I felt when I lifted the slab in the cellar and raised my lantern to behold four pairs of boots standing around, one pair of which I recognised as being of standard police pattern.

In his account of our arrest, Dr. Watson writes of the revolver that was struck from my hand by Sherlock Holmes' hunting-crop. It is true that I was carrying a revolver, but what Watson fails to mention is that it was unloaded. Archie was also carrying an unloaded pistol. The idea was to frighten any possible opposition, not to harm. I have to laugh at the idea that Sherlock Holmes' action here was heroic, as Dr. Watson makes it out to be.* As it was, I was chagrined that we had been snared so easily. I urged Archie to fly, but of course the place was surrounded.

As to the words that Dr. Watson records me as uttering (" I'll swing for it ! "), it was ridiculous for me ever to dream that I should be hanged for an offence such as this. What I actually said was, " I'll sing for you," meaning that I would confess and take all the blame on myself, in the hope that a clean and full confession would mitigate his sentence—as indeed it did.†

---

* Note in Watson's handwriting: " I am sure that Holmes would never have struck Clay in this way had he known Clay was virtually unarmed. However, he had previously been described to us as a murderer, and we beheld a revolver in his hand. I feel that Holmes may be excused his action here."

† Note in Watson's handwriting: " I am sorry that I seem to have misheard Clay and thereby misjudged him. It was obvious at the time that he was encouraging his confederate's escape,

Inspector Jones proved to be something of a sport. I humorously complained of his treatment of me, asserting my blue blood, and he responded in kind. As we rode together in the police hansom to the station, he engaged me in conversation, and given the circumstances, I could hardly have wished for a more amiable companion. Of course, I could have wished for more friendly and favourable conditions, but I pride myself that one of my strengths is knowing when to stop. There was little advantage to be gained in struggling, or even protesting, and so I made an effort to be as pleasant as was possible, and I am glad that he responded in kind.

As I had promised Archie, I took as much of the blame as was possible when I made my confession to the police. I also mentioned my founding of the orphanage, which caused some hilarity at the time among the police to whom I related the story, but I later discovered that they had taken the trouble to verify my tale, and had even spoken with the Reverend Roundhay, who had confirmed my words. Inspector Jones, who told me of this, gave a most comical imitation of that worthy's apparent consternation at being told of my arrest. Also, to his credit, I believe that Inspector Jones took it upon himself to brief my defence counsel—retained by Moriarty, naturally—on the facts of the orphanage. Certainly, I never spoke about it to him, and I am sure neither Moran nor Moriarty would have done so, but it was mentioned as part of my defence plea. I bear neither

---

and given the sight of the revolver as he made his way through the trap, it was natural to assume that Clay was attempting to shoot, and possibly commit murder, for which crime he would certainly have been hanged."

Inspector Jones nor the police any ill-will in this affair. He was only doing his job, as I was doing mine.

At the time of my arrest and during the confinement leading up to my trial, I wished I could have met and spoken with Sherlock Holmes regarding the processes that led to my arrest, but after reading Dr. Watson's excellent account in the *Strand Magazine*, I feel that I am now sufficiently enlightened on that score. However, Sherlock Holmes and I did see each other again, though I confess my view from the dock of him in the witness-box was a little limited.

And now I end my tale. I have had bad news from the doctor. Bad, that is, if I wish to continue living. But, do you know, I am not sure that I do want that. I have had a short life, maybe, but it has been of interest. More money has passed through my hands in a few years than many of my readers will see in their lifetime. I have known many women, and I believe I have made them happier for my knowledge of them. I have had friends among the nobility and among the gypsies, and it is hard for me to tell you which of them I prefer for company. And I may recall that I have been the direct source of happiness for not a few children.

A good life ? Maybe it has not been such, by your standards. But since you will never see me again, at least in this life (and who knows what will be in the next ?) I take this opportunity to stand before you and take my last bow.*

---

* Editor's note: Did Watson read this and remember the phrase ? We have to wonder at the coincidence.

About the Author

HUGH ASHTON came from the UK to Japan in 1988 to work as a technical writer, and has remained in the country ever since.

When he can find time, one of his main loves is writing fiction, which he has been doing since he was about eight years old.

As a long-time admirer of Sir Arthur Conan Doyle's famous detective, Sherlock Holmes, Hugh has often wanted to complete the canon of the stories by writing the stories which are tantalizingly mentioned in passing by Watson, but never published. This latest brings Sherlock Holmes to life again.

More Sherlock Holmes stories from the same source are definitely on the cards, as Hugh continues to recreate 221B Baker-street from the relatively exotic location of Kamakura, Japan, a little south of Tokyo.

Look for Hugh's other books:
Tales From the Deed Box of John H. Watson MD
More from the Deed Box of John H. Watson MD
Secrets from the Deed Box of John H. Watson MD
The Darlington Substitution
and
Tales of Old Japanese
(all from Inknbeans Press) as well as his novels:
Beneath Gray Skies
At the Sharpe End
Red Wheels Turning
All available as paperbacks and ebooks from fine booksellers everywhere. See http://hughashtonbooks.info
Contact Hugh at hashton@inknbeans.com.

More from Inknbeans Press

If you enjoyed this book, you may also want to look at the following titles:

Declaration of Surrender (Book 1 of the Nick West Series)

by *Jim Burkett*. Believing either Germany or Japan is about to win the war against the United States in early 1945, several members of Congress conspire to protect their own wealth by secretly creating a document that would give the rights of ownership of all U.S. properties and land over to the leading country before the end of the war is actually declared.

Signed by the President, the document is passed along underground to the Germans but is eventually confiscated back by U.S. Treasury agents along with account ledgers worth millions of dollars sitting in hidden Swiss bank accounts. Days later the agents are found murdered and the documents gone.

DHS agent Nick West is thrust into the world of government assassins and sought after for treason by his own country when he discovers the location of the missing sixty-five year old document but refuses to disclose its whereabouts in order to protect his own men.

Out of Touch

by *Rusty Coats*. Coats' debut novel, *Out of Touch*, follows a reluctant psychic who feels more burdened than gifted: able to see the past, present and future of those who touch an object before he holds it in his hand. Most of the events and emotions that pass through him like electricity are insignificant and benign, but there are those moments when he experiences the fear, horror and pain of catastrophic events, and even knowing when, where and how these catastrophes occur, his knowledge is useless to prevent them, pointless to protect the victims, nothing but pain and guilt for him. Until now.

An Unassigned Life

by *Susan Wells Bennett*. Frustrated novelist Tim Chase just thought of the best plot idea he has had in three years. The problem is he's dead.

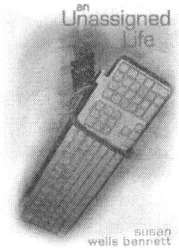

Now he's stuck in the afterlife as an unassigned soul with two goals in mind: getting his last and greatest novel published and moving on.

Why can George see me? he thought. Pulling the El Pad from his pocket, he read the answer:

Some living humans, particularly those suffering from a chemical imbalance of the brain, are able to see and interact with you. Unfortunately, this imbalance frequently leads others to label these individuals as insane.

Great, he thought. If I want to hang out in an asylum, I can have all the company I want.

Yes, answered the El Pad.

INKNBEANS PRESS

INKNBEANS PRESS is all about the ultimate reading experience. We believe books are the greatest treasures of mankind. In them are held all the history, fantasy, hope and horror of humanity. We can experience the past, dream of the future, understand how everything works from an atomic clock to the human heart. We can explore our souls, fight epic battles, swoon in love. We can fly, we can run, we can cross mighty oceans and endless universes. We can invite ancient cultures into our living room, and walk on the moon. And if we can do it with a decent cup of coffee beside us...well, what more can we ask, right?

Visit the Web site at www.inknbeans.com

Fresh Books Brewed Daily

Printed in Great Britain
by Amazon.co.uk, Ltd.,
Marston Gate.